## CHRISTMAS SPECIAL

# The Spirit of Sunnyside

*Look for More Fun and Games with*
**CAMP SUNNYSIDE FRIENDS**
*by Marilyn Kaye*
*from Avon Books*

MARILYN KAYE is the author of many popular books for young readers, including the "Out of This World" series and the "Sisters" books. She is an associate professor at St. John's University and lives in Brooklyn, New York. Camp Sunnyside is the camp Marilyn wishes that she had gone to every summer when she was a kid.

## CHRISTMAS SPECIAL

# The Spirit of Sunnyside

## Marilyn Kaye

AN AVON CAMELOT BOOK

CAMP SUNNYSIDE FRIENDS CHRISTMAS SPECIAL: THE SPIRIT OF SUN-NYSIDE is an original publication of Avon Books. This work has never before appeared in book form.

AVON BOOKS
A division of
The Hearst Corporation
1350 Avenue of the Americas
New York, New York 10019

Copyright © 1992 by Marilyn Kaye
Published by arrangement with the author
Library of Congress Catalog Card Number: 92-93067
ISBN: 0-380-76921-2
RL: 5.1

First Avon Camelot Printing: October 1992

CAMELOT TRADEMARK REG. U.S. PAT. OFF. AND IN OTHER COUNTRIES, MARCA REGISTRADA, HECHO EN U.S.A.

Printed in the U.S.A.

OPM 10 9 8 7 6 5 4 3 2 1

For Rebecca Burstein

# Chapter 1

Erin sat propped up on a bed in her room at the Carlyle School. A pad of paper rested on her knees. She was making her Christmas list. She'd finished noting down the gifts to buy for her mother and father, her grandparents, her girlfriends, and the housekeeper. Now came the fun part—choosing the gifts she wanted for herself.

Chewing on her pencil, she considered the possibilities: jewelry, perfume, clothes, a portable compact disc player . . .

Her roommate, Ann, came in dragging a suitcase. Erin raised her eyebrows. "You haven't started packing yet? We're leaving in just a couple of hours."

"I don't have that much to pack," Ann said. "Unlike *some* people," she added with a grin.

Erin gazed at her own red leather luggage, bulging at the seams and stacked on the floor. She'd retrieved the luggage from the school storage room a week ago, and she'd started packing almost immediately. "We're going home for three weeks," she reminded Ann.

Ann opened a drawer and began pulling stuff out. "Yeah, and I'll probably wear the same jeans every day," she said cheerfully. "That's one of the great things about vacations. You can be a slob."

Erin had a feeling her own vacation and Ann's would be very different. "Are you and your family doing anything special over the break?"

"We always have a lot of fun," Ann told her. "On Christmas Eve, we go caroling with a bunch of people from the neighborhood. All my relatives get together on Christmas day, and later, we'll help out with the party at the nursing home where my grandmother lives. What about you? Anything special planned?"

"My mother's inviting my cabin mates from Camp Sunnyside to stay for the week before Christmas. She's calling their mothers today."

"That sounds like fun," Ann said. "What are you guys going to do?"

"Shop," Erin said promptly. "A new shopping center just opened up near my home, and it's supposed to be the biggest mall in the state. I'm glad it opened in time for Christmas." She indicated the pad in her lap. "I'm making a list of what I

2

want so my parents and my other relatives will know what to get me."

"Do you want to know what you're going to get?" Ann asked. "I prefer surprises."

"Not me," Erin said. "If people are going to spend money on me, they might as well get me what I want. Returning gifts is such a drag."

Fran and Karen, their friends from across the hall, came in. "Just wanted to say good-bye," Fran announced. "We're taking the next bus to the train station."

"What are you guys up to?" Karen asked.

"I'm packing," Ann told them, "and Erin's making her Christmas wish list."

Fran peered over Erin's shoulder and gaped. "You're expecting all that?"

Erin studied the list. She didn't think it was all that extravagant. "What are you going to ask for?"

"I'm keeping my fingers crossed for a stereo," Fran announced. "I've been hinting like crazy."

"I want ice skates," Karen said. "And I'm hoping for a cordless phone. I love talking on the phone, but I hate sitting still while I'm doing it."

"A cordless phone!" Erin exclaimed. "I hadn't even thought of that!" Quickly, she added it to her list.

Ann gazed at her curiously. "Will you really get everything you ask for?"

"Probably not," Erin admitted. "But the more I ask for, the more I'm likely to get."

3

Ann sighed. "If I ask for too much, I get a lecture on being greedy. Between me and my sisters and my brother, at least one of us gets that lecture every year." She giggled. "My mother says it's becoming one of our Christmas traditions!"

Everyone laughed, but Ann's remark got Erin thinking. She knew her roommate's family was not wealthy. With five kids in the family, Ann probably didn't get too many Christmas presents. An idea occurred to her, and she added a note to her list. *Gifts I get that I don't want—bring to Ann.*

Then she smiled, feeling good about her thoughtfulness. Since this was her first year away at school, she knew her parents were really missing her. Because of that, she anticipated a particularly fine Christmas this year, a real onslaught of presents. Maybe Ann would benefit from that too.

Sarah Fine burst into the house, with her stepsister, Trina Sandburg, close at her heels. Normally, they tried to be quiet when they returned from school, since Trina's mother worked at home. But today they had big news, and they couldn't wait for her to take a break.

"Laura! Laura!" Sarah shouted, while at the same time, Trina was yelling, "Mom! Mom!"

Mrs. Fine came running out of the kitchen. "What's wrong? What happened?" The fear on her face vanished when she took in the expressions on the two girls. "Good news?" she asked.

4

"Good news?" Trina exclaimed. "It's great news! It's fabulous!"

Sarah was hugging herself and hopping up and down. "I still can't believe it!"

Trina's mother had her hands on her hips. "Well, would one of you please inform me what this good, great, fabulous, unbelievable news is?"

"Tell her," Trina ordered Sarah.

Sarah tried to look modest, but it was impossible. "I won the state junior high essay contest!"

Her stepmother gasped. "Darling, that's wonderful!" She threw her arms around Sarah. "I'm so proud of you!"

"It was announced over the intercom at school this morning," Trina reported. "I was so excited I practically screamed!"

Sarah laughed. "You were excited? You should have seen me. I was in a state of shock!"

"And in English class, the teacher made her read the essay aloud," Trina added. "Everyone clapped."

"It was a little embarrassing," Sarah noted.

Trina grinned. "Come on, you loved it."

"Yeah," Sarah said. "You're right." They both started giggling.

"You worked hard on that essay," Trina's mother stated. "You deserve to get applause."

"That's not all she got," Trina said. "Show her, Sarah."

"There was a prize." Sarah extracted an envelope from her bag and pulled a check out. Trina's mother's eyes widened.

"Two hundred dollars!"

"What are you going to do with it all?" Trina asked.

"I don't know," Sarah said. "I've never had so much money before."

"I'm sure Erin will have some ideas about how you can spend it," Trina's mother noted.

Trina and Sarah looked at her in puzzlement. "Erin?" Trina asked. "What does she have to do with this?"

"Her mother called this morning. She's inviting all the cabin six girls to visit the week before Christmas and Hanukkah."

The girls let out a whoop, and Mrs. Fine smiled. "I guess I don't have to ask if you want to go. Mrs. Chapman told me that a new shopping center opened near their home, and that Erin thinks it would be fun to have all the girls there to shop for gifts together."

"I bet Erin will want to do some *serious* shopping," Trina said. "And you'll have the money to buy Hanukkah gifts, Sarah."

"Having money is nice," her mother agreed. "But what I'm really excited about is Sarah's essay. It's a great honor, Sarah."

Sarah nodded. "I can't wait till Dad comes home so I can tell him."

"Why don't you call him at work?" Trina's mother suggested. "Good news like this shouldn't have to wait. And I think I'll go make a cake. We should have a celebration tonight." She took off for the kitchen.

"I'm going to change," Trina said. She started up the stairs.

"Trina, wait." Sarah went to the foot of the stairs and beamed at her stepsister. "You're terrific."

"Why?" Trina asked.

"Some sisters . . . well, they might be jealous. But you're acting like you're just as happy as I am."

"I *am* just as happy as you are," Trina replied immediately. "And I'm not jealous. It's not as if we were competing in the essay contest!" She blew Sarah a kiss. "I'll be back in a minute."

Sarah went to the phone and dialed the hospital where her father worked. "Could I speak to Dr. Fine, please?"

While she waited for the connection, she thought about that two hundred dollars. What *would* she buy with it? Delicious ideas floated through her head. Fancy cowboy boots were the latest fashion trend at school. She'd been admiring a classmate's pair just the other day and wishing she could afford them. Or maybe she should get her ears pierced and buy an entire wardrobe of earrings. There were so many possibilities . . . money was wonderful! And she'd still have plenty for Hanukkah presents.

Upstairs, Trina thought about Sarah's great honor as she changed into jeans. No, she wasn't

7

jealous, not a bit. Writing was Sarah's talent. Trina wouldn't mind winning an award someday herself—but for her *own* talent. Of course, she didn't really have a talent yet, but she did have a new hobby. And if she worked on that hobby, she just might turn it into a talent.

She wandered over to her desk, where the results of her hobby were spread out. They were photographs. Not the ordinary kind of photos, like the ones people took of each other. These were artistic photographs—bare trees decorated with tufts of snow, birds flying across a winter sky. . . . Trina examined them closely. She didn't think they were bad for a beginner.

She'd only become interested in photography recently. Just last month, her stepfather had taken her and Sarah to a museum where there was a special exhibition of photography. Trina had never before thought of photographs as art. But when she saw the exhibit, she realized that an artist could use a camera instead of a brush.

Ever since that day, she'd been fascinated by photography. She took her old camera everywhere, just in case she saw something that would make a nice picture. She'd joined a photography club at school, and she had signed up to take classes at the Y in January.

But as she took her camera out of her bag, she sighed. How could she ever expect to take truly artistic pictures with such an ordinary camera? Reading the photography magazines and talking to others in the club, she'd become aware of all the fancy cameras a person could use to take really professional pictures.

She had planned to ask for a camera as her main Christmas gift, and she'd gone to look at some in a camera shop. When she'd seen the prices, her heart had sunk. She'd had no idea they cost so much. How could she possibly ask for such an expensive present?

She opened a desk drawer, pulled out a box, and started counting the money she'd been saving from her allowance and baby-sitting. She figured she had about half the money she needed for the camera. Maybe she could ask for the rest of the money as an early Christmas gift and buy her camera when she and the girls were at Erin's.

She wrinkled her nose. Money as a Christmas gift didn't seem right. But oh, how she wanted that camera!

Megan Lindsay and her friends, Krista and Lori, were sprawled on the floor of Megan's bedroom. While her two friends went through Megan's cassettes, Megan flipped through the latest issue of her tennis magazine.

Suddenly, she shrieked. Krista went pale and Lori dropped a tape. "What's the matter?" they cried out in unison.

"This is it!" Megan screeched. "Right here!" She jabbed her finger at the magazine page.

"Oh." Krista groaned. "Tennis stuff."

But Lori, who was Megan's regular Saturday tennis partner, crawled over to see what Megan was so excited about.

"This is what I want," Megan told her. "Isn't it absolutely gorgeous?"

"Awesome," Lori agreed.

Their enthusiasm drew Krista closer. "Let me see." She examined the advertisement in the magazine. "What's the big deal? It's a tennis racket."

"It's not just any tennis racket," Megan told her. "It's *the* tennis racket. It's a new kind, and it's supposed to be the best racket in the world."

Lori confirmed this. "All the famous players are using it now. I'm getting one for Christmas."

Megan looked at her in surprise. "How do you know?"

"Because I asked for it," Lori replied.

Krista's eyes widened. "You came right out and told your parents what to get you?"

"Sure," Lori said. "How else could they ever know what I want? I always make sure they know exactly what to get me for Christmas."

"Wow," Megan said in awe. "My parents would never let me do that. They believe that Christmas gifts should be surprises." She giggled. "Like I'm supposed to think they still come from Santa Claus."

"My parents are like that too," Krista said. "But I'm lucky. All I want this year is clothes, and my mother's got great taste. She knows exactly what I like."

10

"Not mine." Megan sighed. "They mean well, but last year I got that awful tennis outfit, the one with the frilly ruffle on the skirt." She shuddered. "It's amazing what they can come up with. But I could never tell them exactly what to get me. They're always going on about the real meaning of Christmas, and how people shouldn't make a big deal out of the gift-giving part of it."

"You should get this racket," Lori said. Her eyes gleamed wickedly. "Otherwise, I'll have a major advantage in our Saturday games."

"You'll have to do some serious hinting," Krista advised Megan.

"That's silly," Lori scoffed. "You know what I did last Christmas? My parents and I went to the mall. I showed them exactly what I wanted and they bought it. Then they wrapped everything up, and I pretended to be surprised on Christmas morning."

"That doesn't sound very Christmassy," Megan commented.

Lori shrugged. "Come on, what's Christmas really all about, anyway? Look, how many times a year do we get big presents? On our birthdays and Christmas, right? Megan, if you don't get that racket now, you'll have to wait till your birthday."

"And that's not until September," Krista pointed out.

Megan agreed. "Maybe I can find more ads like

11

this, and I'll leave them all over the house. They *have* to get the message!"

"Guys, we need to plan some shopping trips," Lori said. "I've got so many gifts to buy people, I should get started right away."

"Me too," Krista chimed in. "Let's go this weekend. Megan, can you go?"

"I can go," Megan said slowly, "but I won't have any money to spend."

"Your parents haven't given you money to buy gifts yet?" Lori asked.

"No, and they won't." Megan bit her lip. "They'd never let me run around with real money. They still think I'm a little kid, and I'd spend it all on something silly."

"You still don't get an allowance?" Krista asked.

Now Megan was really embarrassed. "No. Whenever I need money for something, like movies, I ask for it. And they always give me exactly the right amount. I guess they just don't think I'm old enough to manage my own money."

"How do you buy Christmas gifts for other people?" Lori asked.

"My father goes with me to buy my mother's gift," Megan told her. "My mother shops with me for everyone else's."

Lori pointed a finger at her. "Megan, if you want to be treated like an adult, you have to act like one. There's one big difference between adults and kids. Adults have money. Since we're not old enough to have jobs, they have to *give* us the money."

Megan had never thought about it like that. And after her friends left, she kept on thinking about it. Maybe it was time for her to have her own money, to spend the way she wanted to spend, without having her parents' approval.

She wandered into the kitchen where her mother was feeding her baby brother. "Mom, can I talk to you about something important?"

"Of course, Megan," her mother said, but just that minute, the phone rang. Megan took the spoon from her mother's hand and started feeding Alex while her mother picked up the phone on the kitchen wall.

"Hello? Why, hello, Mrs. Chapman. How are you?"

Megan's head jerked up. The only Mrs. Chapman she knew was the mother of her friend Erin from Camp Sunnyside. The spoon holding baby food was frozen in midair as she turned.

"Is that Erin's mother?" she asked. Mrs. Lindsay put a finger to her lips. Meanwhile, baby Alex was frantically beating his hand at the spoon. Megan turned her attention back to him, but every few seconds she cast an anxious eye toward her mother. The last time Mrs. Chapman had called was to invite Megan to join Erin on a trip to Italy.

"What a nice invitation," Mrs. Lindsay was saying. Megan's heart leapt.

"Invitation to what?" she asked excitedly. Her mother frowned and put a finger to her lips again.

"Of course, I'll have to discuss this with my husband. Could I call you back this evening?"

Alex let out an outraged cry. Megan turned back to see that she'd just hit his cheek with a spoonful of creamed corn. Quickly, she wiped it off before her mother could see. Her mother was still talking.

"Yes, we're fine. Yes, it has been unusually warm for this time of year. No, it doesn't look like we'll be having a white Christmas."

Megan groaned. Were they going to have a long discussion about weather predictions now?

Finally, her mother hung up the phone. "What is it?" Megan asked. "What's going on?"

Her mother hesitated. "Well, I should talk to your father first—"

"Mom! At least tell me what it's all about! Are we having another Sunnyside reunion?"

Mrs. Lindsay sat down at the table. "Here, give me that spoon before you drown Alex in baby food. Yes, it's a reunion. Mrs. Chapman is inviting all the cabin six girls to visit during the week before Christmas."

Megan let out a whoop. Then she noticed little wrinkles forming on her mother's forehead, a sure sign that she wasn't exactly thrilled about this idea. "What's the matter?"

Her mother sighed. "Well, I'm not too happy about the way Mrs. Chapman described the plans for the week. It seems that Erin wants you girls to join her for a Christmas shopping spree at a new mall that's opened there. I don't know that I'm crazy about the idea of young girls running around a shopping center buying Christmas gifts on their own."

"Mom, we're not that young," Megan protested. "And it's about time you and Dad let me shop on my own."

Mrs. Lindsay frowned slightly. "I suppose Mrs. Chapman will be with you, so you won't be completely on your own."

Privately, Megan doubted that. She knew Erin shopped on her own all the time. But she didn't say anything about that. "Mom, please!"

"Well, I'll talk to your father."

Megan grinned. She could tell from her mother's tone that she'd give in. And her father would go along with it.

A Christmas shopping spree! Sunnyside buddies, no adults or counselors to follow around, money in her pocket, and a chance to prove to her parents that she knew how to handle that money. And when her parents saw how well she did that, maybe they'd start letting her do that all the time.

There had been other Sunnyside reunions—the trip to Italy, a skiing holiday—and they'd all been fun. But this reunion could have life-changing results for Megan.

\* \* \*

Katie Dillon was counting her money. She'd been putting some aside from her allowance every week for months—well, almost every week. And she'd borrowed from this stash occasionally. When she'd finished her calculations, she frowned, and counted again. Her frown deepened.

There wasn't anywhere near as much as she thought there would be. Here she was, getting ready to leave for a shopping spree with her Sunnyside cabin mates, and she didn't even have enough to buy decent gifts for her parents and her twin brothers. Forget about the item or two she might want to get for herself.

She was going to have to ask her parents for more, she decided. She knew there was no way she'd have as much as Erin, who was truly rich. But at least she should be able to keep up with the spending of the others.

"Katie!" Her mother's voice rang out from downstairs. "Supper's on the table!"

She ran downstairs and entered the dining room in time to hear one of her brothers make an announcement.

"Michael and I have decided what we want for Christmas," Peter said to their parents.

"I thought you wanted rollerblades," Mr. Dillon said.

"Oh, sure, we still want those," Peter said. "But there's something else too."

"New bikes," Michael declared.

16

"But you have perfectly good bikes," Mrs. Dillon protested.

"Those are kid bikes," Peter stated. "We need ten speeds."

"And helmets," Michael added.

Katie opened her mouth to announce that if the boys were getting ten speeds, she wanted one too. But something in her parents' expressions stopped her.

"Boys," their mother said slowly, "do you have any idea what ten speed bicycles cost?"

Peter shrugged. "Sure. A few hundred dollars, something like that."

Mr. and Mrs. Dillon exchanged long looks. Not angry ones, though. Their expressions were more like—sad. Suddenly, Katie had the uneasy feeling that she and her brothers were about to hear something very serious.

Their father coughed, and his expression became solemn. "Kids, I think you're old enough now to understand what's going on. You know that the economy isn't very strong right now, and that we're in the middle of a recession."

"You've seen the news on television," Mrs. Dillon added. "There are people in this country who have nowhere to sleep, nothing to eat. . . ."

Katie began to feel nervous. "Are we going to be poor?"

"Oh no, nothing like that," her father assured her. "We're luckier than many people, because we have a home and we can put food on the table.

But people don't have very much money to spend, so the sales at my store have been off."

Mrs. Dillon spoke up, gently. "What your father and I want to say, kids, is that Christmas isn't going to be quite as extravagant this year. You can't expect to get as much as usual."

Crestfallen, Peter asked, "No bikes?"

"Not this year, dear," Mrs. Dillon said. "I'm sorry."

There was a silence at the table. Katie and her brothers looked at each other. Finally, Michael said, "We understand," and at the same time, Peter said, "It's okay."

Katie nodded too. "We'll be happy with whatever we get."

Her mother smiled. "Thanks for not fussing about this, kids. Hopefully, by this time next year, the economy will have picked up, and then we can talk about bikes."

Katie was glad she hadn't mentioned the money she needed for the shopping spree. It would have only made her parents feel worse. She'd have to get by on what she had.

But she hoped her face wasn't revealing what she was thinking. At Erin's, the others would be going crazy, spending and buying. But this wasn't going to be much of a shopping spree for *her*.

# Chapter 2

Erin scrutinized the bare fir tree that stood in the corner of the vast Chapman living room.

"It's a nice full one, isn't it?" her mother commented. "We'll decorate it tonight when your camp friends are here. Did you invite any others over?"

Erin nodded. "Just Claire and Hilary. And Claire's bringing two cousins who are visiting her for the holidays." It was too bad most of her friends had gone away for the holidays, she thought. It would have been nice to have been able to invite some guys, someone she could flaunt as a boyfriend. Claire's cousins were boys, but they were only ten and eleven years old.

"Be sure to tell Ms. Howard so she'll know how many to expect," Mrs. Chapman said.

"Okay." Erin looked around the elegant room with its Oriental rugs, plush furniture, and beautiful ornately framed paintings on the walls. She'd never paid much attention to the room before. In fact, she'd always taken her home for granted. Now, she was trying to see it through the eyes of her cabin mates.

They would definitely be impressed, she decided. She'd been to all their homes, and none of them lived in as grand a house as Erin did. None of them had a real housekeeper, like Ms. Howard, or a private swimming pool. Of course, it was too cold to use it now, but it was there to be seen.

But there was something that bothered her. "I wish you and Daddy hadn't sold the limousine."

"We didn't need it anymore after Mr. Peters retired," Mrs. Chapman replied.

"Then why didn't you just hire another chauffeur?"

Mrs. Chapman looked thoughtful. "To tell you the truth, Erin, I was never comfortable being driven around in that huge car. I always felt like we were showing off. Particularly now, when so many people are having hard times. We're very fortunate to be well-off, but there's no reason to throw our good fortune in people's faces."

Erin didn't understand that at all. What was the point of being rich if you couldn't show off to your friends?

"And besides," her mother added, "I've enjoyed learning to drive again."

"Why don't we have a cook anymore?" Erin asked.

"Because we don't need one," her mother said. "When the cook decided to take another position, your father and I realized that having a cook was an unnecessary extravagance. Ms. Howard and I manage quite well. And I've discovered that I love to cook!"

Erin sighed. A house full of servants would have made her friends' eyes pop out.

"It's time to go pick up Sarah and Trina," Mrs. Chapman announced, putting on her coat.

Erin did the same, and wrapped a scarf around her neck. "When are the others coming?"

"In just about an hour. Katie's parents are picking up Megan."

They went out to the garage, where Erin made a face at the perfectly ordinary station wagon her parents had gotten to replace the limousine. As her mother started the car, Erin said, "Mom, I just remembered something else I want for Christmas. A cordless phone."

Her mother frowned slightly. "Good heavens, Erin, don't you think you've asked for enough?"

"It's Christmas, Mom!"

Her mother had to concentrate on driving so there wasn't much conversation on the way to the bus station. When they arrived, they went inside the terminal.

"I'll go see if the bus is on time," Mrs. Chapman said, and went to stand in line at the information

21

window. Erin looked around. She'd never been in the bus station before.

It looked sort of old and grimy to her, but loops of tinsel on the windows and a lopsided Happy Holidays sign added a small note of cheer.

It was the crowd that gave the bus station more of a festive feeling. Since it was holiday time, there were a lot of people around, waiting for buses to arrive or leave, looking excited and expectant and impatient. Some sat on benches, surrounded by suitcases. Others stood, watching the clock or the door through which travelers would arrive. A general sense of anticipation filled the air.

Erin strolled around the room. She looked at the men and women and children, and wondered where they were going or who they were waiting for. One person in particular grabbed her attention, and held it.

He sat on a bench, and he looked neither excited nor impatient. He was just staring into space, through the greenest eyes she'd ever seen in her life. Erin had always loved green eyes.

But this guy had more than that going for him. He was absolutely great looking. She tried not to be obvious as she gave him a once-over. He was at least thirteen, she decided, and maybe fourteen. A shock of straight, fair hair hung down almost to those amazing eyes. He was thin, but not scrawny. He wore the battered, torn-at-the-knees jeans that all the guys were wearing.

Was he coming or going? she wondered. She

didn't see any suitcases by him, just an old knapsack, the kind lots of kids carried around with them everywhere.

Suddenly, their eyes met. Erin was ready to look away quickly, but he smiled. It was a nice smile, sort of shy. Erin smiled back.

Then her mother returned. "The bus is going to be fifteen minutes late," she reported. "Why don't we run across the street. I need to pick up more Christmas cards at the gift shop."

"You go, Mom," Erin said. "I'll wait here."

"Why?"

Erin hoped she hadn't noticed her watching the boy. "Well, um, the bus might come early—you never know. It would be just awful if Trina and Sarah showed up and there was no one here to meet them."

Mrs. Chapman looked around the bustling station uncertainly. "I suppose it's safe to leave you here alone. Just don't talk to any strangers, all right?"

Erin maneuvered a hand behind her back and crossed her fingers. "I won't."

As soon as her mother disappeared, Erin moved casually toward the boy. She looked up, pretending to study the board on which the times of departing and arriving buses had just been changed. The one Trina and Sarah would be on was listed. She faked a look of dismay. "Oh dear," she said out loud.

The boy raised his eyes. "Huh?"

"The bus is late," she said.

"Oh."

She gazed around. "It's busy here, isn't it. I guess because of the holiday . . ."

"Yeah," he replied.

She bit her lip. So far, she was only getting one-word responses. But at least he was looking at her. And she thought he looked interested.

There was an increase in the noise level as a busload of travelers entered the terminal. Some of the waiting people rushed toward them, and the room echoed with cries of greeting.

The boy was watching the arrivals too. "Are you expecting someone?" Erin asked. Not a girlfriend, she hoped.

He shook his head. "No."

"Going away for the holidays?"

"Yeah."

Inwardly, she sighed. He looked like a nice guy. Already, she'd been having fantasies of exchanging names and phone numbers, getting together over the holidays, showing him off to her cabin mates . . . Maybe he wasn't staying away for too long. He couldn't be, without any luggage.

"Where are you going?" she asked.

For a moment, he looked blank. Then he glanced up at the board on the wall. "Cleveland." Then he grinned, revealing straight white teeth. "You ask a lot of questions."

She flushed. "Sorry. I didn't mean to seem nosy."

24

"That's okay," he said. "Now it's my turn. What about you? What are you doing here?"

"I'm waiting for some friends who are coming to visit. We're going to spend the week shopping for Christmas and Hanukkah gifts."

"Nice," he said.

"I haven't even started buying gifts yet," she went on. "Have you?"

"No."

"I love Christmas," she said, "but all that running around, buying presents, it can get exhausting, you know what I mean?"

Before he could respond, a ragged man shuffled by her. "Lady, you got any spare change?"

Erin drew back. "No," she said coldly. The man moved on. Erin was about to express her annoyance, when she noticed the boy watching the man. *He* didn't look annoyed—his expression was more sympathetic.

Hastily, Erin changed her own reaction. "That's so sad, isn't it? It must be terrible to be poor. Especially at Christmas."

The boy nodded. Erin glanced at the door. She saw her mother outside. She didn't want her mother catching her talking to a stranger, even a nice-looking young one. Frantically, she tried to think of some subtle way to leave him with a lasting impression.

But it was too late. Her mother was coming toward her. "Has the bus arrived?"

25

"Not yet," Erin said. Through the window, she could see a bus pulling up. "Maybe this is it now."

They both watched as people stepped off the bus. "Yes, I think I see your friends now," Mrs. Chapman said. She started toward the arrival door.

Erin glanced back at the boy. He was looking off in the opposite direction.

"Come along, Erin," her mother called.

Quickly, Erin unwound her scarf and let it drop to the floor. Then she hurried after her mother.

Sarah and Trina were among the first to enter the station. Sarah let out a squeal that made Erin wince, and she hoped the boy wasn't watching. The girls greeted Mrs. Chapman and hugged Erin.

"Thank you for inviting us," Trina said to Erin's mother.

"It's our pleasure," Mrs. Chapman said. "Now, we have to get right home. Katie and Megan will be arriving soon."

"We're decorating the tree tonight," Erin told them. "I invited some other friends over too."

"This is going to be great fun," Sarah said enthusiastically. "I love Sunnyside reunions! Remember the one we had at Katie's? That was super!"

"You've got a short memory," Trina said, laughing. "Don't you remember falling on the ice when we were skating and spraining your wrist?"

"I guess I forgot that part," Sarah said.

"You don't have to worry about anything like that here," Erin assured her. "We're not doing anything dangerous. All we're going to do is shop."

Mrs. Chapman winked at Sarah and Trina. "I don't know about you girls, but I consider shopping to be one of the most dangerous activities my daughter does! I'm counting on you two to keep her under control, or we'll all end up in the poorhouse."

"Oh, mother," Erin groaned while Sarah and Trina giggled.

They piled into the car, and Mrs. Chapman started the engine. "Mom, wait!" Erin said suddenly. "My scarf is gone. I must have dropped it in the station." She opened the car door and slid out. "I'll be right back."

Back inside the terminal, she looked toward the bench, expecting to see the back of his head. He wasn't there. In despair, she realized his bus must have left.

But then she thought she made out a wisp of fair hair. She ran over to the front of the bench.

He hadn't left. He was still there, in the same place. She hadn't seen him because he was lying down on the bench. He appeared to be sound asleep.

She pondered her next move. Did she dare jot her phone number down and leave it lying beside him? No, anyone could pick it up.

Just then, a booming voice rang out. "Bus for Cleveland, now ready to depart. All aboard, please."

27

That was his bus! Tentatively, Erin reached out a hand and touched his shoulder. The boy's eyes flew open, and he jerked upright, clutching his knapsack tightly.

"I'm sorry," Erin said. "But I just heard your bus being called."

"Oh. Thanks." He got up and stared at the exit, where people were beginning to file out. But he made no effort to move in that direction.

With a little thrill, Erin suspected that he wanted to linger and talk to her some more. But everyone was waiting for her outside in the car. And it wouldn't be right to make him miss his bus.

"You'd better hurry if you want to get a window seat," she said.

"Yeah, right." Slowly, he started toward the door.

He hadn't even asked her name! She couldn't let a cute guy like this just disappear. "Wait!" Erin cried out impulsively. He turned.

"My name is Erin. Erin Chapman. My name's in the phone book." She couldn't believe she was being so pushy! But she couldn't help thinking how super it would be if this guy started calling her while her friends were here.

"I'm Woody. Woody Patterson." And with a smile, he went out the door.

He hadn't said he'd call. But he hadn't said he *wouldn't.* Erin made a mental note to ask her friends about him tonight. This was a small town,

28

and he had to go to one of the two schools in town. Maybe somebody knew him.

She ran back outside and got into the car. "Erin, where's your scarf?" her mother asked.

She'd completely forgotten about it. "Oh, I guess somebody took it. I'll have to buy a new one tomorrow."

Her mother gave her a disturbed look. But before she could reprimand Erin about her carelessness, she turned to the girls in the backseat. "What's new?"

"Sarah won an essay award," Trina announced.

"How nice," Mrs. Chapman said. "What was the essay about?"

Sarah began to tell them, but Erin wasn't listening. Something out the window had caught her eye. It was that boy, Woody. He was walking away from the station.

How strange, Erin thought. Had he missed his bus? Or maybe meeting her had made him change his mind about leaving town! No, even though she thought she was well worth that, it was a pretty conceited thought.

Trina was watching her. "Erin, do you know that boy?"

"No, not really," Erin murmured. But silently, she added, "not yet."

# Chapter 3

"You mean we're not all sleeping in the same room?" Katie's eyes were the size of saucers.

Erin gave her friend a queenly smile. She remembered well the Sunnyside reunion at Katie's house, where they all slept in sleeping bags on Katie's bedroom floor. "There's no reason for us to sleep in the same room here," she stated. "We've got four extra bedrooms."

Megan, too, was in complete awe. "This is the biggest house I've ever seen! It's like a hotel!"

"I could get lost in this place," Sarah murmured. "And that bathroom! It's bigger than my bedroom at home!"

Erin beamed with pride. Her tour of the house had been a great success. She hadn't missed their expressions when she'd pointed out the grand piano, the billiard table, the swimming pool, the wide-screen TV in the den. Sarah and Megan had oohed and ahhed over everything they'd seen, and Trina had been practically speechless.

"Erin," Katie said suddenly, "you're really rich, aren't you?"

"Katie," Trina chided, "you're not supposed to ask people questions like that."

"Besides," Megan added with a grin, "you know the answer to that. We've been listening to Erin brag about all the stuff she has for three summers!"

"I do not brag!" Erin protested indignantly. She led the girls into her bedroom, the room she'd been saving for last. Megan went into a rapture over the canopy bed and the elaborately ruffled matching curtains, while Sarah and Trina gazed in hushed admiration at the walk-in closet.

"You've got your own phone extension," Katie noted.

"It's not an extension; it's my own private line," Erin said. "Of course, it's just a regular telephone. I'm hoping for a cordless one for Christmas."

"I guess you don't have a recession here," Katie murmured.

"How many people are coming to the tree-decorating party tonight?" Trina asked.

"Just a couple of friends," Erin said. "And one of them is bringing her cousins, two boys. But they're too young for us. All the really decent guys I know are out of town." Just then, she had an idea. "I have to make a phone call. Why don't you guys go down to the kitchen? Ms. Howard made brownies."

As soon as they left, she searched her room for a telephone directory. She finally found one, and she opened it to the *P*'s. "Darn," she groaned. There were at least a dozen Pattersons. She ran a finger down the names but there was no Woody. Of course, that didn't mean anything—most kids didn't have their own phones.

She wasn't about to call each and every Patterson in search of him. But maybe she could try one or two, and hope for good luck. She had a perfect excuse for calling—she could invite him to the tree-decorating party.

She dialed the first number, and a woman answered. "Could I speak to Woody, please?"

"There's no one here by that name."

"Thank you." She hung up and tried another. She got the same results. She was about to dial the third number, when there was a rap on the door.

"Come in."

Her mother stood in the doorway. "Erin, your friends are all down in the kitchen."

"I know," Erin replied.

"Don't you think you should be there with them? After all, you are the hostess."

"Okay." She gave one last longing look at the phone. If he was new in town, his family was probably not even listed yet anyway.

32

She found her cabin mates gathered in the kitchen, listening eagerly as the housekeeper described the goodies she was preparing for the party that evening.

"I'm making crab puffs," Ms. Howard told the girls, "and miniature egg rolls and little pizzas, with an assortment of toppings you can add."

"There goes my diet," Sarah said, but without any sign of regret.

Ms. Howard continued. "Of course, there will be the usual chips and dips—" She stopped suddenly and clapped a hand to her mouth. "Oh dear, I forgot to pick up the sour cream for the dip. I'll have to go to the store." She started to take off her apron, glancing anxiously at the clock.

"We could go for you," Trina offered.

Ms. Howard looked at her with a startled expression, and Erin wasn't surprised to see this. *She* never volunteered to run errands for Ms. Howard.

"I couldn't ask you to do that," Ms. Howard protested.

"We don't mind, do we?" Trina asked the other girls.

"Heck, no," Megan said cheerfully. "It will give us a chance to look around the neighborhood."

"Is there a grocery store within walking distance?" Trina asked Erin.

"Yeah, over on Central Street. I'll get money from Mom."

33

"Well, I certainly appreciate this," Ms. Howard said.

Moments later, the five girls were walking along the tree-lined street. "This is pretty," Trina said, admiring the ornate homes they passed. "I can't wait until I get my new camera so I can take some pictures here."

Sarah explained to the others. "Our parents gave her money so she can buy herself her own big Christmas present while she's here."

"Lucky you," Katie said.

Trina looked thoughtful. "I don't know. It feels weird to me, buying my own Christmas present. It just doesn't seem like the way it's supposed to be."

"That's dumb," Erin scoffed. "It doesn't matter who gives you the present as long as you get it. And for once, you'll be able to get exactly what you want."

"That's right," Megan agreed. "Parents are always more generous at Christmas time, and we have to take advantage of that."

They'd just turned a corner when Erin stopped short.

"What's the matter?" Katie asked.

Erin couldn't believe her own eyes. There he was, halfway down the block, the boy from the bus station, Woody. What absolutely amazing good fortune!

"Is that a friend of yours?" Megan asked.

"He looks familiar," Trina said. Then she

snapped her fingers. "The boy you were watching at the bus station!"

"What boy from the bus station?" Katie asked.

"Oh, just some guy I saw . . ." Erin replied vaguely.

"He's cute," Sarah declared. "What's he doing?"

"It looks like he's rummaging in a trash can," Megan said.

"Don't be silly," Erin muttered. But as she watched, she had to admit that was what he was doing. He had a big bulging plastic bag with him. He pulled a bottle out of the trash can, and dropped it in the bag.

"Don't stand here gawking at him," Erin snapped at the girls. She strode down the block, and rearranged her features as she approached him.

"Woody," she said, "what a surprise!"

From his startled face, she knew her appearance was a surprise to him too. He froze, and his grip on an empty soda can tightened. "Oh! You're—Erin, right?"

Pleased that he remembered her name, she nodded. Then she waved a hand to indicate her companions. "These are the friends who are visiting me. Sarah, Trina, Megan, and Katie."

She wasn't alarmed by the fact that his expression became wary. No boy would be comfortable being confronted by five girls. He managed a "pleased to meet you" while the girls mumbled the same.

35

"Did you miss your bus today?" Erin asked.

"Um, no, I just, well, I changed my mind about leaving town," he replied. He put the soda can he was holding into his plastic bag.

In her annoyingly blunt way, Katie asked, "What are you doing?"

"Collecting bottles and cans," Woody replied.

Trina nodded knowingly. "The things that can be recycled."

"That's right," he said.

Erin had no idea what they were talking about. Her face must have revealed this, because Sarah explained.

"Glass and aluminum can be reused. We've been keeping cans and bottles out of the trash at school, and putting them in special bins for recycling."

Erin wrinkled her nose delicately. "But isn't that nasty, taking stuff out of trash cans?"

"It's for the environment," Megan said. "And it's important, because we're running out of land-fills to dump trash in."

"And burning trash puts toxic chemicals in the air," Katie added.

Woody was nodding with approval at their remarks, so Erin nodded too. "Oh, okay. Woody, where are you going to take that stuff?"

"To a grocery store," he told her. "They'll accept recyclable items. Is there one around here?"

"We're on our way to a grocery store now," Erin said to Woody. "Come with us."

He seemed a little reluctant. "You guys go on

ahead. I'll catch up." He dug back into the trash can for the one remaining bottle.

The girls started walking, but Erin lagged behind, so that when Woody caught up with them they were side by side.

"Are you new in town?" she asked him.

"Yes."

"Where do you live?"

He didn't answer right away. Then he said, "We're staying with some people. Till we find our own place."

"Where did you move from?"

He turned and faced her directly. "You're the most curious girl I've ever met." But the smile on his face as he spoke took the edge off the mild insult. Erin decided she wouldn't ask any more questions.

The grocery store they entered was just an ordinary grocery store, but the cabin six girls explored the aisles with interest. Woody went to the cashier with his bag of bottles and cans. Erin considered going with him, but she didn't want to be obvious in her pursuit. Even so, she hurried the girls through the store to collect the sour cream so they'd be sure to meet Woody on the way out.

"Sarah, come on," she urged as Sarah paused before a display of cookies.

"Ooh, I just love these, and they hardly ever have them in the store back home," Sarah moaned.

"Then just get them," Erin ordered.

They made it back to the cashier in time. Woody was just getting his money for the bottles and cans.

"It amounts to two dollars and forty-five cents," the cashier said.

The girls watched as the cashier counted out the money. "That's not much for so much work," Megan noted.

"He wasn't doing it for the money," Trina said.

Sarah paid for her cookies, Erin paid for the sour cream, and they all left the store together. Once outside, Sarah tore open the bag of cookies. "Anyone want a cookie?" she asked.

No one did. She ate one, and then another. Then she let out a heavy sigh. "I shouldn't have bought these. I know I'm going to end up eating them all myself."

"You need to be more disciplined," Trina said mildly. "Just decide you'll have one or two a day, that's all."

"You know that's impossible for me," Sarah said mournfully. "I have no willpower."

"Then there's only one thing to do," Katie declared. "Throw them away."

"It's such a waste," Sarah said. "But I guess you're right." She started toward the closest trash can.

Erin turned to Woody. "We're having a little party at my house tonight, nothing fancy, just to decorate the tree. Would you like to come? There will be other boys there," she added hastily, in case he didn't like the idea of being surrounded by girls.

He didn't even seem to be listening. He was watching Sarah drop the almost full bag of cookies into the trash can.

"What's the matter?" Katie said. "See a bottle you missed?"

Woody went to the trash can and withdrew the cookies. When he turned back, all the girls were eyeing him curiously.

"You never know when you'll run into a hungry person," he said. "I have to go." He started off, walking rapidly in the opposite direction.

Erin gazed after him in disappointment. He hadn't even responded to her invitation.

"He seems like a nice boy," Trina said. "The kind of person who thinks about others."

Except me, Erin thought sadly.

The tree-decorating party was in full swing. While Erin's father unraveled strings of lights, Trina and Megan strung cranberries and popcorn on long threads, assisted by the two boys who had come with Claire. The delicious aroma of Ms. Howard's delicacies and the freshly popped corn filled the air, and there were carols on the stereo. Boxes of carefully wrapped ornaments lay around the tree. Slowly, with each garland of tinsel and every glittering ball, the tree evolved from a bare green fir to a brilliant, dazzling spectacle of color.

Erin's friend Claire scolded her two cousins. "You guys are eating more popcorn than you're stringing."

"Look at these unusual ornaments," Hilary commented, peering into a box.

"They *are* different," Katie agreed. She picked one up to put on the tree.

"Be careful with those," Erin warned. "They're antique handmade ornaments, and very valuable. They're worth hundreds of dollars each."

"I think that's an exaggeration, dear," Mrs. Chapman said.

Even so, just holding one made Katie nervous. "Maybe you better put these on," she said to Hilary. Hilary looked to her like the type of girl who was more accustomed to handling expensive objects.

Katie wandered away from the tree, and gazed around the room. Despite all those days back at camp, when she'd heard Erin describe her life, she was still amazed by the wealth that surrounded her. Amazed and a little depressed.

Hilary and Claire joined her at the table laden with food. "I love Christmas," Hilary said. "Sometimes I think my parents are so stingy, but at Christmas they make up for it."

"What are you getting?" Claire asked.

Hilary smiled happily. "A horse."

Katie stared at her in disbelief. "A real live horse?"

Hilary laughed. "Well, I wouldn't want a dead one."

"I was hoping for diamond earrings," Claire said. "The dangling kind. But my parents said no."

"Too expensive?" Katie asked.

"No, they say I'm too young for long earrings. I'll probably just get studs."

Katie moved away to where Megan and Sarah were separating thin strands of tinsel. Sarah was talking excitedly. "I can't wait to hit those stores tomorrow with real money in my purse! For once, I can get my family really nice Hanukkah presents. And even have some money left over for myself!"

"I'm still floored that my parents gave me so much money," Megan said. "I've been counting it every night!"

"What are you going to buy, Katie?" Sarah asked.

"Don't know," Katie murmured. All she knew was that it wouldn't be much, not compared with what the others would be purchasing.

"Doesn't the tree look gorgeous?" Trina asked. "It makes me feel so Christmassy!"

"Have you tried those crab puffs?" Sarah rolled her eyes in ecstasy.

Megan began to sing along with the record playing. " 'Deck the halls with boughs of holly . . .' " The others joined in.

Katie just stood there, with a fixed smile that was beginning to hurt. Yes, the tree was beautiful, the music was nice, the food was fabulous. But how could she feel Christmassy when she was broke?

# Chapter 4

"That was fun last night," Trina said as Ms. Howard placed a huge tray of steaming French toast on the breakfast table in the kitchen.

"We'll have even more fun today," Erin stated. "We're going to shop till we drop! You know, there are supposed to be almost two hundred stores in this new mall."

"Wow!" Megan's eyebrows shot up to the tip of the curls on her forehead. "That's kind of scary."

Katie gave her a puzzled look. "What do you mean, scary? What's scary about stores?"

Megan explained. "Well, let's say I see something I want to get for my mother in one store. I'll be afraid to buy it in case I see something I like better in another store."

Erin eyed her in disdain. "Haven't you ever

heard of returns? You can always bring whatever you buy back to the store and get your money."

"Two hundred stores," Trina murmured. "How can we go to two hundred stores in one day?"

"We don't have to hit all of them today," Erin said. "That's why I invited you guys for a whole week. We can go to the mall every single day."

"Every single day?" Katie groaned. "We can take a break and do something else once in a while, can't we?"

"Well, maybe," Erin conceded.

Her mother came into the kitchen. "Good morning, girls." She gazed around the table. "Somebody's missing. Where's Sarah?"

There was an instant response to her question. A sleepy-eyed Sarah drifted into the kitchen. Her movements were slow and listless, and Mrs. Chapman eyed her in concern. "Didn't you sleep well, dear?"

Sarah barely had time to get her hand to her mouth before the yawn slipped out. "I always have a problem sleeping my first night in a new bed," she admitted. "I just read until I fell asleep."

"How many books did you read?" Trina asked. "Ten?"

Sarah smiled weakly. "Two. That's all I brought with me." She turned to Erin. "I hope there's a bookstore in this mall."

"I'm sure there's every kind of store in this mall," Erin said with assurance. "But I hope

43

you're not planning to spend all your prize money on books!"

"There's nothing wrong with spending money on books," Mrs. Chapman remonstrated. "But, Sarah, there's a library just a few blocks from here. You can use my card and check out some books if you like."

"Thank you, Mrs. Chapman," Sarah said.

"But we have to go to the mall," Erin objected. "The stores open at ten!"

"I don't think it would matter if you got there at eleven," Mrs. Chapman noted. "I sincerely doubt that the stores will sell out of everything in an hour."

Erin pouted slightly, but she knew her mother was right. "What time can you take us there, Mom?"

"I'm afraid I can't drive you today. Your father's car wouldn't start this morning, so he had to take mine."

Erin's dismay increased to despair. "Mom!" she wailed. "How are we going to get to the mall?"

Mrs. Chapman spoke briskly. "There's a bus at the corner that goes directly there."

Erin gazed at her in horror. A bus! She couldn't remember the last time she'd been on a bus. Oh, *why* did her parents give up the limousine?

None of the other girls seemed bothered at the notion of a bus, but Mrs. Chapman could see the unhappiness on Erin's face. "Erin, come here."

Erin joined her at the counter, where her

mother rummaged around in her pocketbook. "Here's a little extra money. Treat yourself to something nice." She pressed some bills into Erin's hand.

Erin beamed at her mother and kissed her cheek. A little pouting could produce amazing results! From the corner of her eye, she could see Katie watching, her upper lip curled. Katie was always telling Erin she was spoiled.

Erin didn't care. Katie might be right, but Erin didn't mind being spoiled at all. She pranced back to the table and helped herself to French toast.

Katie tried to give Erin a narrow-eyed look, but Erin wasn't paying attention. She's getting more money, Katie thought glumly. And money continued to be the main topic of conversation at the table.

Trina was telling Megan about her shopping plans. "My parents told me I could use all the money on a really good camera, but I'm hoping to find a bargain. That way I can get really nice presents for my family."

"I want to find bargains too," Megan said. "This is the first time my parents have given me money to spend on my own. I have to show them I can handle it properly."

Sarah had been eating rapidly, and she cleaned her plate first. Rising from the table, she asked, "Anyone want to go with me to the library?"

"I'll go," Katie said promptly, even though she hadn't finished eating. She'd do anything to get

45

away from all these reminders of how everyone had more money than she did.

Mrs. Chapman gave Sarah her library card, and the girls got their coats. "Don't take too long," Erin called after them. "We want to start shopping."

"Shopping, shopping, shopping," Katie complained as she and Sarah left the house. "I'm sick of that word. That's all anyone can think about around here."

Sarah spoke in a matter-of-fact tone. "Well, that's what we've been invited here to do. Funny, I never used to like shopping. But now that I've actually got real money to spend, it's different."

"Money," Katie grumbled. "Shopping and money. That makes two words I'm getting tired of hearing. Can't we talk about something else for a change?"

When Sarah didn't answer right away, Katie turned to face her. Sarah was gazing at her curiously. "Katie, is something wrong? You don't seem like you're in a very good mood. It's not like you to gripe so much."

Katie was silent for a few moments. Then, she let her worries out. "Erin says we're going shopping every day for a week. I can guarantee you that it won't take me longer than fifteen minutes to spend all the money I've got." She told Sarah what her parents had told her and her brothers, about the recession and how they shouldn't expect a lot of presents for Christmas.

Sarah was immediately sympathetic. "Gee, that's too bad. Katie, I hope you don't mind my asking this, but has your family become, you know, poor?"

Katie shrugged. "My father says we're not, but I'm starting to feel like I am." Feeling abashed, she admitted, "I'm even feeling jealous of Erin."

"Oh, Katie, that's silly," Sarah said. "Erin might be rich and beautiful, but that's not everything. She doesn't really have anything else, like a hobby or a talent. Think of all the things you're good at that she's not."

"All I can think of is the money she has that I don't," Katie said.

"Well, at least libraries are free," Sarah said as they went up the steps to the building.

That wasn't a particularly cheering thought to Katie, since she wasn't much of a reader. Inside the library, Sarah went to the young adult paperback rack and became engrossed in picking out books. Katie wandered over to the magazine rack, selected one, and began to leaf through it.

That didn't entertain her for long. The magazine was filled with holiday gift suggestions. Katie stuck it back in the rack and picked another one. This one was no different. The pictures made her feel sick.

She looked around for some other way to amuse herself. There weren't many people in the library that morning, but she was struck by one boy leaning back in a chair, a magazine in his lap.

47

Katie recognized him immediately. It was the boy who had been collecting the bottles and cans, Woody. Maybe she could spend time chatting with him, about the environment, or anything that had nothing to do with money or Christmas.

She moved toward him, but as she got closer, she realized his eyes were closed. "Woody?" she called softly. There was no response. He appeared to be sound asleep.

Sarah came up to her. "I checked out my books, we can go now."

Katie put a finger to her lips and nodded toward Woody. Sarah's eyes widened in recognition. "Is he sleeping?"

Katie nodded.

Sarah looked at her watch. "At ten-thirty in the morning?"

Katie shrugged. "I always get sleepy when I'm reading." She grinned. "We should let Erin know he's here. I think she likes him."

Sarah giggled. "Yeah, information like this would be just about the only way to get her into a library."

They left and started back to Erin's house. They were halfway there when Katie spotted something on the ground. "What's that?" She bent down and picked up a red leather object.

Sarah examined it with her. "It looks like some sort of fancy wallet. Someone must have dropped it."

Katie opened it. "Look at all these compart-ments." Each one of them had a zipper.

"Maybe there's an identification card in one of them," Sarah said.

Katie tried one compartment. There was no identification card in that one. What *was* in there made Katie gasp. "Look at all this money!"

Sarah poked through the bills, and took in a breath sharply. "I've never seen hundred-dollar bills before! And there's a bunch of them! How much money is there?"

Katie looked around nervously. "A lot. I don't think we should count it right here on the street." She closed the wallet and put it in the inside pocket of her jacket. "Let's wait till we get home."

"Katie!" Sarah was obviously shocked. "You're not thinking of keeping that wallet, are you?"

Katie smiled wistfully. All that money . . . what wonderful things it could buy! "No, of course not. I'm sure there must be a name inside. If not, I'll ask Mrs. Chapman what to do."

They continued walking. "I knew a girl who found an envelope full of money once," Sarah said. "There was no identification inside, and she turned it in at the police station. But no one ever claimed it, so she got to keep the money."

Katie wished Sarah hadn't told her that. She didn't want to get her hopes up.

"Of course," Sarah continued, "she had to wait months before the police gave up looking for the owner."

Well, there's nothing to get excited about then, Katie thought. If she had to wait months, it would be too late for Christmas shopping anyway.

Still, she was just a tiny bit disappointed when they got back to Erin's, and found an identification in one of the little zippered compartments. The card held a name, an address, and a phone number. Katie showed her find to Mrs. Chapman.

"I'll call this Ms. Armstrong right away," Erin's mother said. "I'm sure she'll be very happy to hear her wallet's been found." Katie concentrated on thoughts of Ms. Armstrong's relief. It made her feel a little better.

"Come on, everyone," Erin said urgently. "Let's go."

They were putting on their coats when Katie remembered the boy in the library. The excitement over the wallet had made her forget. "Erin, guess who we saw in the library? That boy from yesterday, Woody."

Erin stared at her in disbelief. "You're kidding! In the *library?*"

"Even cute guys read sometimes," Sarah noted.

"Who is this Woody?" Mrs. Chapman asked.

"Just a boy I met," Erin said casually. "He's new in town." But as soon as her mother was out of earshot, her nonchalance disappeared.

"Okay, guys, we're going to make a little side trip to the library on the way to the bus stop," she announced.

"I hope he's not still sleeping," Sarah whispered to Katie as they left the house.

Katie smirked. "It doesn't matter. If he is, Erin will wake him."

As they neared the library, Erin called the procession to a halt. "Maybe I should go in alone. He might not like the idea of a bunch of girls chasing him."

Megan grinned, her eyes twinkling. "But just one would be okay, huh?"

Katie folded her arms across her chest. "What are we supposed to do while you're in there flirting?"

"You'll just have to wait," Erin stated.

But that turned out not to be necessary. Just then, Woody emerged from the library. "Let me handle this," Erin hissed. But Woody noticed them right away and ambled toward them.

"Gee, this *is* a small town," he said. "I'm running into you guys everywhere."

Erin smiled brightly. "How do you like our library? Isn't it nice?"

"How would *she* know?" Megan whispered to Katie. But Katie was more interested in Woody's response. He wore the oddest expression, like he wanted to be there talking to Erin, and he didn't want to be there, at the same time.

"Yes, it's nice," he said.

Sarah gazed at him curiously. "Why didn't you check out any books?"

"I don't have a library card," Woody replied.

"You should get one," Sarah said. "I'm sure they're free here."

"That doesn't have anything to do with it," Woody said quickly.

Sarah seemed somewhat taken aback by the sharpness of his response. Woody flushed. "I mean, the reason I don't have a card is because I don't have a permanent address. Yet." He seemed very anxious to change the subject. "Are you guys going in the library now?"

"No," Erin said. "We're on our way to the bus stop, so we can go to the new mall. Would you like to come with us?"

"To the bus stop?" he asked.

"And to the mall," Erin said.

He didn't answer, but he started walking with them. When they got to the bus stop, he said, "I have to go now. Maybe I'll run into you again."

"Come with us," Erin urged.

He looked torn. Then he put his hand in his pocket. Taking it out, he said, "I can't. You have to have correct change for the bus."

"I've got plenty of change," Megan piped up.

"I can't take your money," he objected.

"You can pay me back when you get some change," Megan said.

He shook his head. "I don't like to owe money."

Erin was getting very frustrated. Suddenly, she brightened. "Woody, you'd be doing me a big favor if you'd come with us."

"What do you mean?" he asked.

52

She smiled prettily and cast her eyes downward as if she was a little embarrassed. "You see, I don't ride buses very often, and they make me a little nervous. There are so many weird people around. We really need an escort."

Katie looked at Trina and rolled her eyes. "Is she nuts?" she whispered. "Does she think he's going to believe that five perfectly healthy eleven-year-old girls can't take care of themselves on a bus?"

But Woody actually bought Erin's act.

"Well, I guess I wouldn't be a very nice guy if I refused," he said.

"Oh, thank you, Woody," Erin gushed. Just then, the bus pulled up, stopped, and the doors opened.

"Unbelievable," Katie murmured to Sarah as she watched Woody take Erin's arm and lead her up the steps to the bus.

Sarah nodded. "I guess I was wrong."

"Wrong about what?"

"It seems that Erin really does have a talent after all!"

# Chapter 5

The new mall was a true shopper's paradise. On three levels, shops surrounded open courtyards where hordes of people milled about. There were restaurants, too, and a complex of movie theaters.

All over the enclosed area, fancy decorations and sparkling lights celebrated the season. A gigantic golden Hanukkah menorah stood in the center of the mall. Christmas songs poured forth through unseen loudspeakers. Signs in the windows proclaimed sales, discounts, and special prices that guaranteed everyone the best holiday ever.

Everyone except Katie. Even with the sales and bargains offered by the shops, Katie could see right away that she wasn't going to be able to afford the kind of gifts all the other girls were talking about buying.

For a while, the girls just wandered, peering into windows and admiring this and that. Erin somehow managed to stay a few steps behind the others, and Woody stayed by her side.

Megan was entranced by a store featuring leather goods, and plastered her face at the window.

"Ooh," she crooned. "Maybe I could get my father leather gloves."

Sarah joined her to examine the goods. "I'll bet Laura would like a real leather wallet."

Katie watched and listened with envy. She'd seen the prices in front of the gloves and the wallets. Trina sidled up beside her.

"I would have thought Erin would be the one going crazy here. Look at her."

Katie didn't have to. She knew Erin would be focusing all her attention on Woody. "It figures," she said. "If there's one thing Erin likes better than shopping—"

"It's boys," Trina finished. She gazed at Katie in concern. "Why do you look so gloomy?"

Katie decided there was no point in burdening Trina with her woes. There was nothing Trina could do about it. "Oh, it's nothing. I just don't know what to get anyone for Christmas. There's my father, my mother, the twins . . . do you think it would be okay if I got the twins one thing that they could share instead of separate gifts?"

55

"Sure," Trina said. "What did you have in mind?"

"I don't know."

Trina cocked her head. "How about one of those electronic game things? All the boys I know are crazy about them. Look, there's an electronics store. I'll bet they've got those games." She turned to the others. "Let's go over there."

"I want to see these gloves up close," Megan said. "Let's go into the leather store."

Erin spoke up eagerly. "You know, we don't have to stay together the whole time while we're shopping. We could separate and meet up somewhere later."

The others exchanged knowing grins. It was obvious to all of them why Erin was so quick to suggest this. But Katie couldn't resist a little teasing. She pretended to look thoughtful. "Let's see, how should we split up?"

"Oh, it doesn't matter," Erin said in a too-casual tone. "Megan and Sarah want to look at leather stuff so I guess they should stick together. And you and Trina want to go to the electronics store, so you guys could shop together."

Katie nodded slowly. "Which leaves you with— Woody!"

Erin faked surprise. "Oh! That's right." She turned to him. "Is that okay with you?"

Woody grinned and nodded. He didn't seem at all displeased with this proposal.

The girls agreed to meet for lunch at a Mexican

restaurant they'd seen, and they separated. Katie and Trina went to the electronics store.

"This is where I wanted to go anyway," Trina confided in Katie. "I want to look at the cameras."

Inside the store, Katie headed over to a display of electronic game contraptions. In front of the different items, the prices were displayed.

A saleswoman approached her, and spoke. "Can I help you with something?"

"No, thank you," Katie replied. Of all the games on the table, there was only one she could afford. But if she bought it, she wouldn't have a dime left for gifts for anyone else. And she couldn't get one dumb game for the entire family to share.

With her shoulders slumped, she dragged herself over to the counter where Trina was examining some cameras a salesman had laid out for her.

"That's it!" Trina said excitedly. "That's the one I want! Oh, Katie, isn't it magnificent!"

It looked just like a camera to Katie, but she mustered up some enthusiasm. "Yeah, it's great."

"It's got everything I want, even a telephoto lens," Trina said. She looked up at the salesman. "How much does this one cost?"

When he announced the price, Katie whistled. Trina went pale. "That much?" she whispered.

"Maybe you can find it cheaper somewhere else," Katie suggested.

"No, she won't," the salesman stated. "We have the lowest prices in town."

Katie could see that Trina was agonizing. She

pulled her aside. "Of course, he's going to *say* that. He wants you to buy it here."

The salesman must have had very good hearing. He didn't seem the least bit offended by Katie's comment, and he smiled as he shook his head. "No, young lady, you're wrong. See?" He pointed to a sign on the wall and read it aloud. " 'Lowest prices in town, guaranteed.' "

"What does that mean?" Katie asked.

The salesman told them. "If you can find this camera at a lower price in any other store, we will refund the difference to you."

"That certainly sounds fair," Trina said. But the creases on her forehead deepened as she studied the camera again. "It's still so expensive. . . ."

"We do carry less expensive cameras," the man said. "Of course, they won't come with all these attachments, and they don't have the same capabilities."

"So get a cheaper one," Katie said to Trina.

Trina's hand caressed the camera. "But this is the one I really want."

Katie was getting impatient. "Well, if you don't have enough money, you can't get it, and that's that."

"Actually, I *do* have enough money," Trina admitted.

Katie was stunned. "You do?"

Trina nodded. "Between what I've saved from my allowance, and the money my parents gave me to buy my own gift, I can afford the camera."

Just then, Erin and Woody came into the store. They joined Trina and Katie at the counter.

"What are you looking at?" Erin asked.

"Trina's thinking about getting this camera," Katie told them. "Her parents are letting her pick out her own Christmas gift."

Woody looked at the one Trina was holding. "That's a nice camera."

"Do you know anything about photography?" Trina asked him.

"A little," he said.

"What kind of camera do you have?"

"Well, I don't have one now." He took the camera from Trina's hand. "I wouldn't mind one like this."

"Why don't you ask your parents for one for Christmas?" Erin suggested.

He didn't answer. Handing the camera back to Trina, he asked, "How much is it?"

When Trina told him, his eyes widened, and Trina nodded. "Yeah, I know, I feel the same way. It's awfully expensive. I've got enough, but . . ."

"Then buy it," Erin said.

Trina bit her lip. "If I buy this for myself, I won't have very much money for everyone else's presents. Like, I was going to get my mom a bottle of the perfume she likes. But I don't think I'll be able to afford it if I get the camera."

"You can always scrimp on the other gifts," Erin said. "Maybe there's a talcum powder with the same fragrance as the perfume. Powder doesn't cost as much."

"What were you planning to get Sarah?" Katie asked.

"I was thinking about a book," Trina replied.

"Make it a paperback," Erin advised. "They're pretty cheap."

"Cheap," Trina repeated with a grimace. "Christmas isn't a time to be cheap."

"Look," Erin said sternly, "your parents gave you the money to buy yourself a gift. This is the one you want. So buy it. And don't worry about how much you have left for buying presents. After all, it's the thought that counts, right?"

Katie could tell Trina was struggling. She knew Trina wasn't the selfish type. "Trina, your parents are encouraging your photography, right? And they gave you money to buy your own gift, right? They'll be upset if you spend the money on them instead of on the camera. You don't want to upset them, do you?"

"No. I guess you're right." But she looked extremely uncomfortable as she reached into her pocketbook for her wallet.

Erin turned to Woody. "You should write down the brand and model of the camera, so you can tell your parents which one to get you."

"Yeah, I will," Woody said. "Maybe later."

"Okay, but remember, there are only eight shopping days left till Christmas," Erin warned.

Woody just smiled. He didn't appear to be terribly concerned about that.

"Megan, make up your mind!" Sarah said impatiently.

They stood before a rack of packages containing fancy stationery. Megan picked one up, and put it back. Then she picked up another.

"I can't decide," she moaned. "There are so many different ones. And I'm not even sure I want to get my aunt stationery at all. Do you think that's a nice gift?"

"It depends," Sarah said. "Does your aunt write a lot of letters?"

"I don't know," Megan replied. "But stationery's the right price. See, I've got it all figured out, mathematically." She pulled a piece of paper from her pocketbook. She indicated numbers on it. "See, this is how much money my parents gave me to buy presents. I have to buy six presents, for my parents, my baby brother, my aunt, my uncle, and my cousin. So I worked out a formula."

"Why couldn't you just divide the amount of money by six?" Sarah asked.

"Because I don't want to spend the same amount on each gift. I want to spend more on my parents."

Sarah's forehead wrinkled as she examined the elaborate formula. "This looks weird."

"It's algebra," Megan informed her. "The teenage girl who lives next door to me helped me do this."

Sarah pointed to a number off to the side of the others. "What's that for?"

"At the last minute, my dad gave me a little extra money, to buy something for myself." She frowned.

"What's wrong with that?" Sarah asked.

Megan scratched her head. "How will I know what to get for myself when I don't know what they're going to get me?"

"I thought you said they were getting you a tennis racket," Sarah reminded her.

"Yeah, but they might get me other stuff too."

Sarah groaned. "Megan, you're giving me a headache."

"I've got to do this *right,*" Megan stated. "I've got to show them I know how to handle money."

Sarah picked up a box of stationery. "This design is very pretty."

"Yeah, it is," Megan agreed, taking the box from her. She looked at the price tag. "But it's a dollar more than I planned to spend on my aunt."

"So just subtract a dollar from what you're planning to spend on someone else," Sarah suggested.

Megan shook her head. "If I start messing around with these numbers, I'll go crazy." She replaced the stationery. "What are you going to buy everyone?"

"I'm never going to get around to buying anything if you're going to spend all day looking at stationery. Megan, you haven't bought anyone anything yet! Now, are you going to get stationery for your aunt or aren't you?"

"I don't know." Megan brightened. "Let's go to that store we passed and look at the scarves."

Sarah rolled her eyes, but she agreed. They were on their way out when she stopped suddenly. "Ooh, check out this."

"What is it?" Megan asked.

"A desk set! You get all these things to put on your desk so everything can be organized. See, this is for pens and pencils, and here's where you can stack paper, and this thing is for filing computer disks. Wow, look at all these things. There's a place for stamps, and for envelopes. . . ."

Megan sniffed. "It smells like real leather."

"I think it is." Sarah looked at the price. "Yeah, definitely. Boy, would I love to have something like this for my desk."

"You've got all that essay prize money," Megan said. "Why don't you buy it?"

"Because I was going to buy presents for everyone else first, and then see how much I had left over before I bought anything for myself."

Megan looked doubtful. "By the time you get through all your other shopping, this desk set might be gone."

Sarah rubbed her forehead. "Now I'm giving myself a headache."

Megan nodded sympathetically. "Christmas can do that to people."

"So can Hanukkah." Sarah sighed.

Walking along with Woody, Erin kept up a constant stream of chatter. She *had* to, because he didn't say much at all.

"I go to the Carlyle School," she told him. "It's all girls, which is kind of a drag, but I've got some neat friends. Where do you go to school?"

"Well, like I told you, we just moved here. Do you want me to carry some of those bags for you?"

"Thank you," Erin said. "But you'd better think twice before you offer again! I've still got tons of gifts to buy. I haven't even thought about what I'm going to get my father. Every year I get him a tie, because I can't think of anything else. What are you getting your father?"

"I don't know." There was a strained look on his face that was becoming familiar. Erin thought it was best not to ask any more questions.

They were passing a toy store. Woody stopped and looked in the window.

"I'll bet you have a little sister," Erin said.

She was relieved when he nodded. Finally, he was letting her know *something*.

"That doll's perfectly adorable," Erin agreed. "Why don't you get it for her?"

"Maybe I will," he murmured, but he made no move to enter the store.

"What about your mother? What are you going to get her?" she asked.

"Didn't you tell your friends you'd meet them at twelve-thirty?" he said suddenly.

Erin looked at her watch. "Yeah, I guess we'd better get over to the restaurant." They started in that direction, and Erin kept glancing at him. There was something mysterious about him, especially the way he clammed up every time she asked him about his family. Maybe he wasn't on very good terms with them, she thought.

The others were waiting for them at the Mexican restaurant. Trina was clutching the bag containing the camera, but the others weren't carrying any packages at all.

"What's the matter with you guys?" Erin demanded. "Haven't you done any shopping?"

"Megan can't make up her mind about anything," Sarah reported.

"What about you?" Megan asked. "I haven't seen you buy anything either."

"What about you, Katie?" Erin asked.

"I can't make up my mind either."

"Let's eat," Megan said. "Maybe I'm just too hungry to make decisions."

"I hope I'll be able to eat," Trina said. "Spending all that money on the camera has made my stomach all jumpy."

The group sat at a large round table and studied the menu posted on a big board.

"Yum, tacos," Sarah said.

"What's the difference between a regular taco and a taco supreme?" Megan asked.

"There's probably more fattening stuff on the supreme one," Sarah replied.

Erin contemplated the menu. "I can't make up my mind between an enchilada and a tostada." She smiled coyly at Woody. "Which do you think is better?"

"They're both good," Woody said.

"What are you going to have?"

A girl wearing a multicolored poncho and a big sombrero came up to their table. "Hi, what can I get you?" Her pencil was poised over her order pad.

"Two chicken tacos," Megan announced.

"Same for me," said Sarah. "And guacamole."

"Guacamole is fattening," Erin noted.

Sarah sighed. "Never mind the guacamole."

"I want a cheese enchilada," Erin declared.

"A beef burrito for me," Katie said. "And we all want Cokes, right?"

"And what about you?" the waitress asked Woody.

"Nothing for me, thanks."

The waitress walked away, and everyone stared at Woody in surprise. "Why didn't you order?" Erin asked.

"I'm not hungry," Woody replied.

"How can you not be hungry?" Megan demanded. "It's lunch time."

"I had a late breakfast," Woody said.

"That wouldn't make any difference for me," Sarah commented. "I'm always hungry."

Trina gazed at Woody anxiously. "Listen, if you don't like Mexican food, we can go somewhere else."

"No, I like it." His voice became testy. "I'm just not hungry, okay?"

The waitress reappeared with six sodas, and placed them on the table. Woody looked at his in alarm. "I think you made a mistake. I didn't want a Coke!"

"You're not even going to drink anything?" Erin asked.

Woody shook his head and handed the soda back to the waitress. She returned a few minutes later with a tray laden with food.

The girls began talking about what they were still planning to shop for. Woody didn't join in, and Erin began to feel more and more uneasy. Maybe this wasn't such a good idea, dragging him along when he wasn't even hungry, making him sit there while everyone else was eating, forcing him to listen to all this girl talk.

And yet, even though he didn't say anything, he didn't seem to mind listening. In fact, he seemed intrigued by their conversation, especially when they got off the subject of shopping and on to actual Christmas day plans.

"We have a lot of traditions," Katie said. "On Christmas Eve, we go caroling in the neighborhood, and all the neighbors invite us in for treats.

And my mother always reads 'The Night Before Christmas' while we hang up stockings. She's been doing that ever since my brothers and I were babies. My brothers always make faces when she starts, but they listen. Then we wake up at the crack of dawn and run downstairs to see what's under the tree." She stopped suddenly, and seemed to be lost in her own thoughts.

"We always have pecan pancakes on Christmas morning," Megan said. "And then all our relatives come over for a gigantic dinner. Turkey and all that stuff."

Trina turned to Sarah. "You know, this will be our first Christmas as a real family. We'll have to come up with our own new traditions."

Erin tried to bring Woody into the conversation. "Does your family do anything special for Christmas?"

"No, not really."

"I'm stuffed," Megan said. "I can't even eat that other taco."

Woody looked at the untouched taco on the plate. "Do you think I could take that home . . . for my dog?"

"Sure," Megan said, passing the plate across the table toward him. "I'll ask the waitress for a doggie bag."

"You shouldn't give a taco to a dog," Katie objected. "It's not good for dogs, food that's too spicy."

"My dog will eat anything," Woody said. "He likes spicy food."

"You think he'd like these refried beans, too?" Erin asked.

"Sure."

The waitress put the food in a bag for Woody, and after they paid they left the restaurant. They walked past the movie theater complex. "I've been wanting to see that," Sarah said, pointing to one of the posters.

"Maybe we can come back here tonight," Katie said. "Could we, Erin?"

"Sure!" Erin thought it was a great idea. She could finagle a way to sit away from the others, alone with Woody. "Want to come to the movies with us tonight?" she asked him.

"Uh, no thanks, I've already seen that movie," he said.

"There are four other movies playing," Sarah pointed out. "I wouldn't mind seeing any of them."

"I've seen them all," Woody said. "I've got to go now."

"Woody, wait!" Erin hurried after him. "Could you meet us again tomorrow?"

He hesitated. "You really want me too?"

She nodded, in a way that she hoped sent him a message. He must have received it, because he smiled. "Yeah, okay. Where and what time?"

"Right here, in front of the theater. At noon. We'll go somewhere for lunch."

"I have to be somewhere else at lunchtime," he said. "Make it two o'clock, okay?"

"Okay." She watched as he walked away. Then she went back to her friends. "I think he likes me."

"Oh, Erin, you think every guy likes you," Katie sniffed. "He wouldn't even come to the movies tonight."

"Because he'd already seen them all," Erin pointed out.

"That's impossible," Katie said. "Look." Two of the movies had signs over the posters that read OPENING TONIGHT.

"Well, he's meeting us here tomorrow, so there," Erin stated. "Now, come on, let's do some more shopping."

By the time the girls got back to Erin's that afternoon, they were all carrying bags. Katie was feeling even more irritable than she had before. Here her arms were aching from carrying packages, and they weren't even hers!

"Well, it certainly looks like you girls had a successful day," Mrs. Chapman said.

Erin shot them all a fierce look, and no one told Mrs. Chapman that almost all the packages were Erin's.

"And we're going back tomorrow for another successful day," Erin said. "Why, we didn't even get to half the stores!"

Katie managed to hold back a groan. She had

this vision of day after day, trudging around the mall ... by tomorrow, surely the others would start spending their money. And she'd have to watch them.

"Let's go up to my room," Erin said, but Mrs. Chapman stopped them.

"Girls, I've got some news. I called Ms. Armstrong."

"Ms. who?" Erin asked.

"The woman who lost the wallet I found," Katie reminded her. She turned to Mrs. Chapman. "Was she happy?"

"Yes, very relieved," Mrs. Chapman said. "She came over right away to pick it up. And she left this for you, Katie." She handed Katie an envelope.

Probably a thank you note, Katie thought. The girls went upstairs to Erin's room. Everyone sat around and watched as Erin showed off all her purchases.

"Tomorrow, I'm definitely going to start buying things," Megan declared.

"Me too," Sarah echoed.

Katie wondered if there was any way that she could get out of going back to the mall. It was going to get embarrassing, with everyone else buying gifts she couldn't afford, and asking her why she wasn't getting anything for anyone. Maybe there was something like a dime store in this town. That would be about the only place where she could afford to buy presents.

"I'll bet that Ms. Armstrong was thrilled to get all that money back," Trina said. "Katie, why don't you open that envelope and read us what she says?"

Katie tore the envelope open. There was a note inside—but that wasn't all.

The others looked up at her sharp intake of breath. "What's the matter?" Megan asked.

Katie read the note in a shaky voice. " 'Thank you very much for finding my wallet and contacting me. Please accept this little reward for your efforts.' " Her hand trembled as she pulled out a wad of bills.

The girls watched in stunned silence as Katie counted the bills. Finally she looked up, and in a dazed voice, she announced, "It's not so little."

# Chapter 6

Katie was in high spirits as the girls waited for the bus the next morning. Hopping up and down, she entertained the others with an off-key rendition of "Jingle Bells."

"Are you trying to warm up?" Sarah asked. The temperature had dropped quite a bit since the day before, and there was a real chill in the air.

Katie shook her head, and merrily continued hopping and singing.

"Sounds like someone's finally got the Christmas spirit," Trina remarked.

Katie laughed merrily. "It's a lot easier to feel the Christmas spirit when you've got money. Gee, the whole world looks different to me today! I can't wait to get to the mall. I'm ready for shopping!"

"Maybe you can encourage Megan to start shopping too," Sarah said.

"Look who's talking," Megan replied. "You haven't bought anything yet either. Trina's the only one who's had the guts to spend any money."

Trina objected to that. "What about Erin?"

"I'm not counting Erin," Megan teased. "She's always shopping."

When Erin didn't come back immediately with one of her usual retorts, Katie asked, "What's your problem? Did you run out of money?"

"Money isn't everything," Erin replied.

Four mouths dropped open. Katie slapped the side of her own head. "I think something's wrong with my ears. Did I just hear Erin Chapman say that money isn't everything?"

Sarah stepped backward. "Watch out, you guys. I think Erin's body has been taken over by an alien invader."

"Don't tease her," Trina said. "I think she's really unhappy."

Erin nodded. "I am. I just don't understand why Woody didn't call me last night."

Megan looked at her in bewilderment. "Why would he call you last night? You were with him practically all day yesterday, and you're meeting him again today."

"You wouldn't understand," Erin replied. "When a guy really likes a girl, he calls her."

"Maybe he was busy," Sarah said. "Did you *ask*

him to call you? Did you give him your phone number?"

Erin moved her withering glance from Megan to Sarah. "Sarah, you don't *ask* guys to call you, they do it because they want to. And my name is in the phone book."

"Maybe Woody's different from most guys," Trina said thoughtfully. "He *seems* different. Sort of . . . I don't know. Mysterious."

*"I'll* say he's different," Katie echoed. "I never heard of a guy who wouldn't eat when he had a chance to. My brothers—just put them near food and they turn into animals!"

"Don't worry, Erin," Sarah said. "He could be shy. Maybe you need to make the first move."

The bus arrived, and the girls got on. Trina sat next to Katie. "Do you have a paper and pencil?" Katie asked. "I want to make a list of everything I'm going to buy today."

Trina fumbled around in her bag. "Sorry, I can't find any paper."

"Oh well, never mind," Katie said. "I'll just get anything I see that I like."

She was true to her word. As soon as they arrived at the mall, she headed directly to the first store they came to, which happened to be a record store. There, she bought albums for each member of her family. Then she went to the men's clothing shop next door, where she bought a tie for her father. The next stop was at the very next store, a lingerie shop, where she bought a lacy slip for her mother.

"Katie, are you going to buy something in every shop at the mall?" Megan asked in wonderment.

"Why not?" Katie replied with a grin. She marched into the sporting goods store, and picked out a couple of baseball caps for her brothers. While she waited at the cash register, she confided in Trina.

"My parents said we wouldn't be having much of a Christmas, because of the recession. Boy, are they going to be in for a surprise!"

Trina smiled slightly, but her eyes were troubled. "Katie, don't you think you're going a little overboard? If you give your parents so many presents, and they can't give you a lot, they might feel bad."

Katie brushed that idea away. "Then I'll just have to buy some stuff for myself!"

By lunchtime, the girls were all lugging bags, and most of them belonged to Katie. Standing in line at the hamburger place and studying the menu, Sarah said, "I can't decide between French fries or onion rings."

"Get both, and I'll treat you to them," Katie announced grandly.

"Why are you being so generous all of a sudden?" Megan asked.

Katie giggled. "Having lots of money helps."

"But you shouldn't just throw it away," Trina

said. "You should be spending it on something important."

"No way," Katie replied. "It's Christmas! Who wants to think about anything important?"

They got their food at the counter and went to a booth. While they ate, Erin kept checking her watch.

"What time are we meeting Woody?" Megan asked.

Erin raised her eyebrows. *"We?"* she inquired, putting an obvious meaning to the word.

Megan didn't get it. "Yeah, isn't he meeting us today?"

Katie cheerfully interpreted Erin's expression. "I don't think it's *us* that Woody's interested in meeting, Megan. And I think Erin would prefer *us* to get lost. Right?"

"Would you mind?" Erin asked sweetly. "I feel like if I could just get him alone, he'd ask me for a real date."

"That's fine with us," Sarah replied. "We'll go to that big department store at the end of the mall. Maybe Megan and I will find things to spend our money on there."

Katie gazed at them reprovingly. "I can't believe you guys are having such a hard time spending money." She gestured toward all her bags. "Look how easy it is! You two just don't have the holiday spirit."

Erin felt like her own holiday spirit would improve considerably if Woody would just give some clear indication that he was really attracted to her. One reason she wanted to meet him alone was because she was afraid he might not even be there, and she didn't want the others to see her being stood up.

But Woody was there, in front of the movie theater, at exactly two o'clock. The battered knapsack was slung over his shoulder. "Hi!" she called brightly.

The smile she received in return to her greeting certainly helped to lift her spirits. She could see he was happy to see her.

"Where are your friends?" he asked.

"Shopping," she replied. She eyed him anxiously. Was he sorry to be alone with her? "I told them to go on without us because . . . because I'm getting a little tired of shopping myself."

The girls would have roared with laughter if they heard her say that, but fortunately Woody didn't know her all that well. And she was pleased to see that he seemed to approve of her comment. "Yeah, I don't much like shopping either," he said.

"We'll just walk around," Erin said. They strolled down the mall. Sneaking peeks at him, Erin could see he was wearing the same clothes he'd had on the day before, including the battered knapsack and the thin jacket. "Is that warm enough for today?" she asked.

"Sure," he replied.

They walked for a while in silence. "Have you

decided what you're getting your family for Christmas?"

"No," he said.

She tried again. "You're lucky to have a sister. I'm an only child. Of course, that's not so bad. I don't have to share anything, and I get everything I want."

"That's nice," he said.

"My friend Katie says I'm spoiled, but I don't think so. Besides, I can't stop my parents from giving me things, can I? Personally, I think Katie's just jealous." She gave him a coy, sideways glance. "I don't understand why girls are jealous of me, do you?"

This time, all she got was a smile. She was beginning to fidget. Here she was, talking and flirting like crazy and getting no response. Maybe if they sat down somewhere, in a quiet place, he'd be more willing to communicate. She noticed a cute little café that seemed to be practically empty.

"You know, I would just *love* a hot chocolate right now," she said. "Why don't we go in there?"

He flushed. "Look . . . I can't stay. I—well, I promised I'd watch my sister."

Erin tried not to let her dismay show. "Oh, you should have brought her with you. I just love children." That wasn't exactly true but she thought it sounded good.

His next words came out in a rush. "I don't want to leave. It's . . . nice being here."

Silently, Erin added the words "with you." He didn't need to say them, though. She could see now that he liked her, he really wanted to be with her. So why didn't he suggest getting together that evening?

Maybe Sarah was right. She'd have to make the first move. "Woody, would you like to have dinner with me tonight? With us, actually," she added reluctantly. She knew for certain that her mother would never let her abandon her guests.

He spoke nervously. "At a restaurant?"

"No, at my house."

"I'd *like* to," he began, "but . . ."

"But what?"

"Well, um, would it be okay if I wear what I have on? I . . . I may not have time to change."

Her eyes swept over his ripped jeans, the frayed sweater. She knew all the boys considered it very cool to look ragged, but surely he could make a little more effort to look presentable, if only to impress her parents.

She was about to say so, but he looked so anxious that she relented. She didn't want to mess this up. "Sure. What you're wearing is fine."

She gave him the address and told him to be there at seven. He nodded and took off. It wasn't a terribly romantic parting, but what else could she expect in the middle of a crowded shopping mall?

Anyway, she was too excited to care. She ran off to find her friends and share the good news. In the department store, she checked in all the areas she thought they might be exploring. To her surprise, she found them in the least likely place—the cosmetics counter.

As she approached, she heard Trina saying, "Katie, I don't *want* a lipstick. I don't wear lipstick."

"But I want to buy you something," Katie said. "It could be a Christmas present. I'll buy one for Sarah and one for Megan too."

Neither of them seemed any more thrilled with the idea than Trina had been. Sarah said, "Katie, we've never exchanged Christmas presents before and we're not going to start doing that now." To Erin, she remarked, "Katie's turned into a shopping monster."

"Well, you can buy me a lipstick if it makes you happy," Erin said hurriedly. "Listen, guys, I've got big news!"

Megan clapped her hands in glee. "He asked you out!" she crowed.

"See, I told you he liked you," Trina said.

"When's the big date?" Sarah asked.

"It's not exactly a date," Erin confessed. "And he didn't exactly ask me out. He's coming to dinner tonight. Oh, I've got so much to do! I have to decide what to wear, wash my hair, do my nails. . . ."

"And maybe let your mother know you've invited him," Trina reminded her.

"Oh, right. C'mon, let's go home."

"But I've still got money to spend!" Katie protested.

"Don't worry," Erin said. "The stores will still be here tomorrow."

Erin paced the living room. "What time is it?"

"Five after seven," Megan said.

Erin's lips were set in a tight line. "I told him seven. He's late."

"Just five minutes," Trina murmured.

Erin marched into the dining room and examined the table. It looked lovely, very elegant with linen napkins, polished silverware, and a beautiful floral centerpiece. Her mother was setting down the water glasses.

Erin eyed them critically. "That isn't the good crystal, is it?"

"Erin, I don't have time to wash the good crystal tonight. These are perfectly nice glasses."

Erin frowned. For all she knew, Woody could come from the kind of family that used good crystal every night.

"Erin, you haven't told me anything about this boy, Woody," her mother remarked. "Where does he live? What do his parents do?"

"I don't remember," Erin said vaguely. She didn't want to admit to her mother that she knew almost nothing about Woody. "Mom, please don't ask him too many questions. Don't treat him like he's on trial."

"Darling, I have no intention of doing that and

82

neither does your father. Besides, I won't have time. I'm fixing dinner tonight, remember." She bustled off into the kitchen.

Erin made a face. When she invited Woody, she'd completely forgotten that this was Ms. Howard's night off. Usually, her family went out to dinner on those nights. But her mother had been taking cooking classes, and she was determined to show off her new skill.

It was too bad, really. Woody might have been impressed with the way the housekeeper waited on them.

She went back into the living room, where Megan was peering through the curtains out the window. "I think I see him! He's walking up the street!"

Sarah and Katie ran to the window. "Get away from there!" Erin shrieked. "He'll see you!" Then she had a thought. "Why don't you guys go into the den? We don't want to look like we're all lying in wait for him." And it would give her a few minutes alone with him.

The girls obeyed, and Erin waited for the bell to ring. When, after a few minutes, there was no ringing, she herself went to the window and peeked out.

Woody was standing out on the sidewalk, gazing up at the house. He made no move to come up the walkway. Erin couldn't understand. The house number was clearly visible on the front door.

Suddenly, he turned away, and started walking

back in the direction from which he'd come. Erin ran to the door and flung it open. "Woody!" she called.

He stopped. Then he turned back, and slowly made his way toward her.

"Why were you leaving?" she asked as he reached the porch.

"I wasn't sure if this was the right house. I couldn't remember the number."

"Come in," Erin urged. "You must be freezing!"

He entered, and gazed around the room. His eyes widened as he looked around the room, but all he said was, "This is a nice house."

"Thank you."

They both stood there awkwardly, and then Mrs. Chapman came into the room. "You must be Woody," she said cordially. Erin noticed her eyebrows go up a bit as she took in his attire, but of course, she said nothing about it.

"It's nice to meet you," Woody said, and he shook hands with Erin's mother.

"Why, your hands are like ice!" Mrs. Chapman exclaimed. "Weren't you wearing any gloves?"

"I forgot them," Woody said.

Mrs. Chapman shook her head in reproof. "I'm surprised your mother would let you out of the house like that. No gloves, no scarf—"

"She didn't see me leave," Woody explained.

"How did you get here?" Mrs. Chapman asked.

"I walked."

"Oh, then you live nearby?"

Erin uttered a silent groan. She should have known her mother couldn't resist a few probing questions. Before she could come up with any more, she said, "Let me take your coat, Woody."

As he slipped off the thin jacket, she noticed a hole in the elbow of his sweater. Personally, she thought he was taking this ragged look a little too far. He gave her the jacket, but he held on to his knapsack.

"Come on into the den," she said. She led him through the double doors where the rest of the girls were gathered. Her father was in an easy chair, reading the newspaper.

"Hi, Woody," the girls chorused, and Mr. Chapman rose to shake hands.

"How do you do, young man?"

"Fine, thank you, sir," Woody replied. "I'm pleased to meet you."

Mr. Chapman nodded with approval, and Erin beamed. Woody's good manners made up for his appearance. Anyone could see he was well brought up.

"Is your family new in town, Woody?" Mr. Chapman asked.

Woody nodded slightly, but there was that pained expression in his eyes again. Oh no, Erin thought, more questions. "Come with me, Woody," she said quickly. "I'll show you around the house."

She took him from room to room. He didn't say much, but of course, boys didn't gush the way girls did. She wondered if his calm acceptance of everything he saw meant that he lived in an even grander place.

Mrs. Chapman called them in to dinner. It was in the dining room that Woody showed a real reaction. Erin realized that her mother's French cooking lessons were paying off. She'd created a fabulous meal.

"That's the biggest chicken I've ever seen," Megan commented.

"That's not chicken, dear," Mrs. Chapman said. "I hope you like it. It's *canard à l'orange.*"

Megan's face was blank. Woody translated. "It's duck with orange sauce. And it looks delicious."

"Why, thank you, Woody," Mrs. Chapman said.

Erin gazed at him in admiration. "Do you know French?"

"Just a little," he replied.

"Did you study it in school?"

He made a little gesture which didn't exactly answer the question. And then everyone was occupied with passing plates and platters.

Everyone began to eat. Woody more than made up for his lack of appetite the day before. "Have some more asparagus," Mrs. Chapman urged. And Woody seemed happy to comply. Erin had never seen a boy eat so much.

Katie whispered in Erin's ear. "He eats more than my brothers. Both of them together."

Erin whispered back, "Maybe he just appreciates fine food. Maybe he likes French food better than Mexican."

But she had to admit that Woody was eating as if this was his first meal in a year. He had seconds on everything.

Without even being asked, Trina got up to help clear the table. "You don't have to do that, my dear," Mrs. Chapman objected.

"I don't mind," Trina said.

Woody rose. "I'll help you." Erin beamed. His manners were sure to impress her parents.

"No dessert for me," Mr. Chapman announced. "I have work to do."

"You have to work tonight?" Mrs. Chapman asked in dismay.

"Yes, I'm sorry. You know that we've opened offices in France, and I have a number of documents to go through. And they're all in French, which means I have to struggle through them with a French-English dictionary."

"I thought your secretary was fluent in French," Mrs. Chapman said. "Couldn't she translate them for you?"

"She quit last week—her husband just got offered a terrific job in Chicago. And there's not one other person in our office who's fluent in French." He sighed deeply. "After the holidays we'll have to advertise for her replacement. I think it's going to be a hard job to fill."

Woody returned from the kitchen in time to hear those last few words. He seemed very interested. "Mr. Chapman, do you think you might have a job for me?"

"For you?" Erin's father was surprised. "What kind of a job?"

"Oh, anything," Woody said. "Like a messenger, maybe."

Mr. Chapman gazed at him quizzically. "How old are you, Woody?"

"Well, I'm just fourteen, but I'm almost fifteen. And then I'll be sixteen . . ." His voice trailed off.

"But what about school?" Katie asked.

"Yes," Mr. Chapman said. "Have you discussed this with your parents?"

"Yes, sir, and it's okay, really."

Mr. Chapman shook his head. "I'm sorry, son, but there are laws. I can't possibly hire someone as young as you are. Maybe when you're sixteen, we can talk about a summer job, or an after-school job."

"All right," Woody murmured in a disappointed voice. "I understand."

Mr. Chapman left the table. There was an awkward silence. Trina made an effort to break it. "How are you and your family spending the holidays, Woody?"

"The usual way," he replied.

Trina tried again. "Sarah said she saw you in the library. Do you go there much?"

"Every morning."

They ate dessert, a delicious pecan pie. Once again, Woody had seconds, and he eyed the last slice longingly. Surely he couldn't still be hungry,

Erin thought. And if he always ate that much, how did he stay so thin?

After dinner, the girls and Woody went into the den to watch a video. During the movie, Woody asked if he could get a glass of water.

"Sure," Erin said, rising.

"No, you stay," Woody said. "I'll get it." He left, and Erin used the remote control to put the movie on Pause.

"Why does he carry that knapsack everywhere he goes?" Megan asked.

"I don't know and don't ask him," Erin instructed.

A moment later, Trina said, "I think I want something to drink too." She walked out.

"Are we shopping again tomorrow?" Megan asked.

"Of course," Erin replied. "Don't you want to? You haven't bought any Christmas gifts yet. And Sarah still doesn't have any Hanukkah gifts."

"I can't think of anything my mom or dad wants," Megan complained.

"Or needs," Sarah added. "Every time I get ready to buy something I can hear my father saying 'don't waste your money on that.'"

"Well, you have to get them *something*," Katie stated.

Just then, Trina walked back in. She didn't say anything, but Erin thought she looked odd. "Where's your drink?"

"I decided I wasn't really thirsty," Trina mumbled.

Woody returned, and they resumed watching the movie. When it was over, Woody said, "I think I'd better go now."

Erin got up. "I'll tell my father. He'll drive you home."

"No thanks," Woody said. "I'm being picked up."

"But how will anyone know where to pick you up?" Erin asked. "You said you forgot the house number."

Woody opened and closed his mouth several times. Finally, he said, "I . . . I knew it before I left home. I forgot it along the way here."

He said good-bye to the others, and Erin walked out of the den with him. "Thank you for inviting me," he said, "and thank your mother . . ."

"Sure, sure," Erin said. They were at the front door now, and this was the time which he should use to ask her out for a real date.

But he said nothing. He opened the door.

Frantically, Erin said, "I hope I'll see you soon."

"Yeah," he replied. "Me too." He looked out. "Here comes my ride. Bye." And he was out the door, closing it behind him.

Erin wanted to cry. What was this guy's problem, anyway? She went to the window and peered out.

There was no car in front of the house. She saw him walking back down the street.

Later that evening, as the girls gathered in Erin's bedroom, she poured out her feelings. "I just don't understand him. Why does he act so mysterious?"

"You've only known each other a few days," Trina reminded her. "People don't tell each other everything about themselves till they know each other better."

"Yeah, but I don't know *anything* about him," Erin complained. "Only that he has a kid sister. I don't know anything else about his family or where he lives or what he was doing before he came here. And why would he say he was being picked up when he was walking home?"

"Maybe he's got secrets," Megan said. Her eyes glazed over, and all the girls knew what that meant. Her fantasies were taking over. "Maybe he doesn't want you to know about him because . . . because he's the son of someone famous! Like a movie star or a criminal!"

"Don't be ridiculous," Erin said automatically. "But he does act like he's hiding something."

Sarah agreed. "There's definitely something strange about him."

"Yes," Trina said quietly. "There is." Something about the tone of her voice grabbed everyone's attention. Unlike the rest of them, Trina didn't tend to gossip.

"Do you know something we don't know?" Katie asked.

Trina hesitated. "I'm only telling you guys this because I'm worried about him."

"Tell us," Erin demanded.

Trina's eyes were dark with concern. "When I went to the kitchen, I saw him ... taking something."

Erin gasped. "The silverware?"

"No. A jar of peanut butter."

"Peanut butter!" the girls cried out in unison.

Trina nodded. "It was on the counter. I saw him put it in his knapsack. He didn't see me."

There was a silence as the girls absorbed this startling information.

"What do you think this is all about?" Megan asked.

Katie got off the bed and began pacing. "Okay, we've got a mystery here. Let's look at the clues. Where did you first see him, Erin?"

"At the bus station."

"Okay. You thought he was going somewhere, but he didn't, so maybe he'd just arrived from somewhere. He wears the same clothes every day. He won't talk about his family."

Sarah picked up on her train of thought. "He doesn't eat when he has to pay, but he eats like crazy when it's free."

"He steals food," Megan added. "And he's looking for a job."

"And he carries a knapsack everywhere he goes," Erin mused. "Like ... like he's got no place to leave it." She clapped a hand to her mouth. "Do you think he's a runaway?"

"That's one possibility," Katie said.

Erin pondered this. It made sense. "Do you think we should tell my parents?"

"Not yet," Katie said. "Not till we find out the truth."

"How are we going to do that?" Megan asked.

"We're going to find him tomorrow," Katie began.

"And confront him?" Trina asked.

Katie shook her head. "No. We're going to follow him."

# Chapter 7

"Don't eat so fast!" The housekeeper repri-
manded the girls the next morning at breakfast.
"You can't appreciate my muffins if you gobble
them."

Katie spoke with her mouth full. "They're great
muffins, Ms. Howard. But we're in a hurry."

Ms. Howard shook her head. "You girls are
turning into shopaholics."

The girls exchanged looks. Erin put a finger to
her lips, but it was an unnecessary gesture. None
of them said a word about their plans.

Mrs. Chapman breezed into the kitchen. "I have
good news for you girls. Erin, your father's car has
been repaired, and I can drive you all to the mall
today."

Once again, eyes met. But this time, Erin knew

an answer was in order. "We're not going to the mall today, Mom."

"Oh? Have you finished your Christmas shopping already?"

"Not exactly . . ." Erin began.

Katie jumped in. "But we need a break."

"I see." Mrs. Chapman's lips twitched. "Yes, I suppose shopping can be pretty exhausting. What do you girls plan to do for your break?"

"We're going to the library," Erin told her.

From her mother's reaction, Erin might as well have said they were going to Mars. "The library?"

"It's a very restful place," Sarah remarked.

Erin kept looking at the clock. The library had been open an hour, and she didn't know how long Woody would remain there. If he left before they got there, they wouldn't be able to follow him.

She was dying of curiosity. Woody might have been a puzzle to her before, but now he was a real mystery. And that made him even more interesting. "Haven't you finished yet?" she asked Sarah impatiently.

Sarah drained the remainder of her orange juice, and the girls got ready to leave. They all put on hats and wrapped scarves around their faces so they couldn't be identified easily. Erin even wore sunglasses.

"We shouldn't *all* go into the library," Katie said as they walked there. "He'll notice us."

"I'll go in," Erin announced.

Katie objected to that. "No, you're the one he'd

**95**

be most likely to recognize. Let me do it. I'd make a better spy than you would."

"How do you know?" Erin retorted.

Katie grinned. "I spy on my brothers all the time."

They'd reached the library. "You guys wait here," Katie instructed. "And stay behind this column."

Heads bobbed in agreement. Katie ran up the steps to the library. Inside, she stood near the doorway and scanned the room. There were only a few people there, and she spotted Woody almost immediately.

As before, he was sitting in a chair with an open magazine on his lap. His head was down, his chin resting on his chest. Even from a distance, she could tell Woody was asleep.

She debated her next move. Should she go out and tell the others? Should she wake him up?

It turned out that she didn't have to make the decision. As she watched, a librarian went over to him and touched his shoulder. Katie moved forward quietly, so she could hear what the librarian was saying to him.

She positioned herself behind a bookcase, peeked through some books, and strained to listen. She saw Woody's head jerk up. The librarian spoke gently. "I'm sorry, young man. But we can't allow you to sleep here every morning. Is there someone we can call for you?"

Katie couldn't hear Woody's response, but she

saw him rise and pick up his knapsack. She waited until he was out the door, and then she went after him.

She could see the girls still behind the column, but Woody didn't appear to notice them as he moved down the steps. Then he started off down the street.

Katie hurried down the steps and joined her friends. "Let's stay right here until he gets to the corner and see which way he turns."

They watched him turn to the left. The girls walked rapidly up the street, and paused at the next corner. From there they could see Woody, a block away, making a right. They ran to that corner.

Trina got there first. "He's going into the bus station," she reported to the others.

"Maybe he's going back home," Megan suggested.

Erin was horrified by that idea. "Without even saying good-bye to me?"

They went to the bus station, and once again, Katie played detective. As soon as she entered the station, she pressed herself against the wall, to avoid being seen. She need not have bothered. With all the holiday travelers bustling about, she was easily hidden from Woody.

She saw him sit down on an empty bench. Then he propped his knapsack in a corner. Using it as a pillow, he rested his head on it and closed his eyes.

He certainly needs a lot of sleep, Katie thought. But he wasn't going to get much sleep in the bus station. A man in a uniform approached him and spoke. A second later, Woody was on his feet. Shoulders slumped, he made his way out of the station. Katie followed.

She found her friends hiding behind a parked bus. "What's going on?" Megan asked. She was watching Woody trudge up the street.

"I think he's looking for a place to sleep," Katie replied. "Come on, let's go."

Again, they stayed a block behind him. Katie walked ahead of the others, and when she reached the corner, she said "Stop." Woody was walking into a low brick building.

The others caught up. "He went in there," Katie said, pointing.

"What's that place?" Sarah asked.

"I have no idea," Erin replied. The girls walked over to the front of the building, which had two doors. There was no name or any other identifying mark on the building.

"What do we do now?" Erin asked.

"We'll have a stakeout, like the police do on TV," Megan said excitedly.

Sarah shivered. "I'm not standing out here all day waiting for him to come out."

Katie considered all possibilities. "Maybe we'd just better go in there and confront him." She approached the door Woody had entered. Before she reached it, a shabbily dressed man came out. "You can't come in here," he said to Katie. "Use the other door."

The girls went down to the other door. "We still can't just walk in," Trina said. "We don't even know what this place is. It might be a club or something you have to belong to."

A woman passed them and went to the door. Sarah called out to her. "Excuse me. Can you tell us what this building is?"

"Why do you want to know?" the woman asked.

"I'm just—just curious," Sarah stammered.

"It's a shelter."

"For runaways?" Megan asked.

The woman's eyes swept the group. "No. For the homeless. Are you girls looking for a place to stay?"

*"Us!"* Erin drew herself up and glared at the woman. "Do we look like homeless people?"

"I don't know," the woman said calmly. "What do you think homeless people look like?"

The girls looked at each other uncertainly. No one had an answer to that.

"Are you here to volunteer?" the woman asked.

"Yes," Katie said suddenly. She figured that was a way to get inside.

"Come on in," the woman said. She held the door open for them. "This is the women's section. Men are on the other side of the building." Inside, there was a small area where another woman stood behind a desk. "Joyce, these girls want to volunteer."

"But they're just kids, Sandy," Joyce objected.

"We need the help," Sandy said briskly. "They've got two arms and two legs each, and that's enough for me." She glanced at the window. "It's supposed to snow tonight, and the temperature is dropping to below freezing. I have a feeling we're going to have a full house. Follow me, girls."

Sandy led them through double doors. The sight that greeted them was strange and unfamiliar. It was a huge room, almost the size of a gym. Along the sides were plain cots. On several of them, women were sitting. Some read, some talked quietly to each other, some just stared into space. They were old and young, all shapes and colors and sizes. They had one thing in common. None of them looked happy.

She turned back to the girls. "Do any of you have experience with children?"

Trina spoke. "I'm a junior counselor at summer camp."

"Good," Sandy said. "Take one of your friends, and go through that door. There are some children in there you can amuse. The rest of you can help me make up some beds and get them ready for the rush tonight."

"Make beds?" Erin asked faintly.

The woman looked her over, and smiled slightly. "Why don't you go back out front and see if Joyce needs some help."

Trina and Katie went through the door the woman had indicated. Four children sat on the floor, staring vacantly at an old television set. Wavy lines covered the screen.

"Hi," Trina said. -

Three of the kids paid no attention to them, but one little girl turned toward them. Trina and Katie got down on the floor. "My name's Trina and this is Katie. What's your name?"

"Colleen."

"What a pretty name!" Trina commented. "How old are you?"

"I'm six. And almost a half." She gazed at the girls curiously. "Do you live here?"

"No," Katie said.

Colleen nodded wisely. "You live in a house. I used to live in a house with my mommy and daddy and my big brother. My daddy went away."

"I'm sorry," Trina said softly. "That must have made you feel very sad."

"Yes," the child said. "And then our house got all burned up."

Katie thought her heart would break. Looking at Trina, she could tell her friend was experiencing the same feeling. "Where's your mommy?" she asked.

"She had to go somewhere today. But she's coming back." A sudden flash of fear appeared in her eyes. "I hope she's coming back."

"I'm sure she is," Trina said reassuringly. "Where's your brother?"

Colleen pointed to the wall, which separated the

men's side of the building from the women's. "He's over there."

Katie and Trina stared at each other. The same thought had occurred to them at the same time. "What's your brother's name?" Katie asked.

They both knew the answer even before the child spoke. "Woody."

Trina rose and looked out the window. "It looks like snow. Maybe we'll have a white Christmas."

"That will be nice, won't it?" Katie said to Colleen. "Santa Claus likes snow."

The little girl shook her head. "It doesn't matter," she said. "Santa doesn't come here."

Smoothing out a sheet, Megan considered the big room. It looked terribly dreary to her. "Why don't you have a Christmas tree?" she asked Sandy. "That would make this place look a lot more cheery."

"Christmas trees aren't a high priority here," Sandy replied. "We've got too many other things to buy. Like food."

Sarah was trying to plump up a thin pillow. "Didn't you say it was going to get very cold tonight? Maybe we should put heavy blankets on the beds."

"We don't have heavy blankets," Sandy told her. "We can't afford them. You see, we don't get enough money from the county to run this place. We have barely enough to pay for heat and electricity. Of course, we do get some contributions from people, but there's a recession on, and people don't have much to give away."

Sarah nodded slowly. "And it's Christmas. I guess people are spending whatever extra money they have on presents."

"Sometimes Christmas is our best time for contributions," Sandy told her. "People think about all they have, and they appreciate their blessings more. And they have more concern for the people who don't have what they have."

Megan kept her voice low. "How do people end up here anyway? Why are they homeless?"

"Different reasons," Sandy replied. "Troubles and problems with money, families . . . there are a lot of ways a person can become homeless."

The other woman, Joyce, stuck her head in the room. "The mail's here," she called to Sandy. "Could one of your kids give me a hand?"

Sandy sent Megan back out to the reception area. There, Erin was standing before a large open box, which appeared to be full of clothes. Joyce's desk held a pile of envelopes.

Joyce spoke first to Erin. "Go through those clothes and separate them by men's, women's, and children's."

Erin eyed the stack with distaste. "They don't look like very nice things."

Joyce's voice held a note of irritation. "They're second-hand donations. I'm afraid people don't contribute designer originals to homeless shelters." She turned to Megan. "You can start opening these envelopes. Hopefully, most of them contain contributions. Address an envelope to each contributor and put one of these cards in it."

Megan examined the card Joyce handed to her. It read "Happy holidays and thank you for your generous donation to the Eighth Street Shelter."

From the corner of her eye, she saw Erin gingerly use two fingers to lift a shirt from the box. "Ick," she muttered under her breath.

Megan began opening the envelopes. The first two were straightforward contributions, but her brow furrowed as she read the note enclosed with the check in the third envelope. "I don't get this," she said to Joyce, and she read her the note. " 'I am enclosing twenty dollars as a Christmas gift contribution in my sister's name. Please send the acknowledgment to her at this address.' "

"Oh, we got those once in a while," Joyce said. "Instead of giving a friend or a relative a gift, people make contributions in that person's name."

Erin looked up. "So the friends don't get gifts?"

"They certainly do," Joyce replied. "They get the gift of knowing they've made life a little brighter for someone who is less fortunate. Girls, you'll have to excuse me. I have to start making sandwiches for lunch. I'll be in the kitchen if anyone comes in."

She disappeared. Erin picked up another item of clothing and groaned. "This is so gross. Can you imagine anyone wearing a sweater like this?"

"If you don't have any sweater at all, it's better than nothing," Megan said.

Erin dropped the sweater in a pile. "This is really depressing. I guess it's just as bad on the men's side. Maybe even worse." She shuddered. "And Woody's in there." She wrinkled her nose. "How can he stand it?"

"I guess he doesn't have a choice," Megan replied.

The door opened and a woman walked in. She stood there uncertainly.

Erin looked her over. Her face was tired, but she was pretty nonetheless. Her hair was neatly combed, and she wore a nice, camel-colored coat.

She's wandered into the wrong place, Erin thought. "This is a homeless shelter," she told the woman.

The woman smiled slightly. "Yes, I know. I've been staying here for a week."

"You don't look like a homeless person," Erin blurted out. Megan winced. Erin certainly wasn't being very tactful. But the woman didn't appear to be insulted. She stroked the front of her coat.

"Luckily, my coat was hanging by the door when my house was burning. I was able to grab it as I got the children out. Excuse me, girls." She went on into the main room.

"That poor woman," Megan murmured.

"And she looks so—so normal," Erin mused.

"So did Woody," Megan said. "So do most of the people here."

105

Erin went back to the box of clothes. She felt like a cloud of gloom was hanging over her head. What was she doing here anyway? She could be at the mall, where everything was happy and cheerful and Christmassy, instead of at this dreary place.

A moment later, the woman came back out to the reception area. She was trailed by a little girl. "Mommy, why do you have to go away again?"

"I have a job interview, honey. The sooner I can find a job, the sooner we can all leave here and move into a place of our own."

A tear trickled down the child's face, but she nodded.

"Now, you go back inside, Colleen, and play with those nice girls," her mother said. The child did as she was told.

"How many children do you have here?" Megan asked.

"Two," the woman replied. There was clear distress in her expression. "Unfortunately, I can't have my son in here with me, since he's fourteen. He's on the men's side."

Erin made a choking sound, and the woman looked at her. "Are you all right?"

"Yes," Erin managed. "Uh, good luck on your job interview."

The woman sighed. "I'll need it. I used to be a French teacher, but I was laid off, and all school budgets have been cut, so there's no chance of getting another teaching job. I'll do anything, clean

**106**

houses, baby-sit, whatever. But no one seems to be hiring. Well, good-bye girls." She left.

"Do you think she's Woody's mother?" Megan asked.

"I bet she is," Erin said. "Are you finished with those envelopes?"

"Almost," Megan said. "Why?"

"I want to get out of here."

A few minutes later, Joyce returned, and soon after that, some of the regular volunteer workers arrived. Joyce and Sandy thanked the girls for their help, and invited them to come back and help out anytime.

"We could go to the mall now," Erin said to the others as they started home.

"Actually, I'm not much in the mood for that," Trina said.

"Me neither," Katie echoed.

Erin was about to propose some other activity, but something about the way the girls were acting made her think nothing would appeal to them. They were all silent, lost in their own thoughts, all the way home. And once they got there, they separated, and each girl went to the bedroom she'd been using.

Alone in her room, Erin sank down on her bed. She wished she could think of a way to cheer herself up. She could go to the mall on her own, of course. Or call one of her local friends. Or put on some music . . . but she had a feeling none of these activities would lift her spirits. What she really wanted to do was get rid of these creepy thoughts that cluttered her mind—the shelter, those sad people . . . and Woody. But she didn't know how to do that.

Maybe eating something nice would help. She wandered out of the room and down to the kitchen. Ms. Howard was taking some freshly baked cookies from the oven, and the smell was enticing. But the aroma didn't make her hungry. It only made her think about how the people at the shelter probably never had homemade cookies like these.

"Where's my mother?" she asked.

"She went out, Erin."

The phone rang, and Erin picked it up. "Hello?"

"Hi, honey. Is your mother there?"

"No, dad. She's out."

"Well, just tell her I'll be late for dinner again. I've got more of these darn documents to translate. And my French seems to be getting worse instead of better. The way this paperwork is piling up, I may not eat dinner on time for a year!"

"Okay," Erin murmured. She was about to hang up, when an idea exploded in her head. "Dad, wait! I think I might have an answer to your problem."

"What problem?"

"Getting home in time for dinner!"

# Chapter 8

Erin hung up the phone and gazed at it thought-fully. Her father had sounded so surprised by her request. Didn't he think she ever thought about anyone but herself?

She leafed through the telephone book and found the number for the Eighth Street Shelter. She dialed, but the line didn't connect, and all she got were odd sounds of static.

Still lost in thought, she jumped when Ms. How-ard said, "Tell your friends there are freshly baked cookies here."

"All right," Erin murmured, but she didn't think they'd be any more excited by the prospect of cookies right now than she was. Emerging from the kitchen into the dining room, she could see

Trina in the living room at the front door. "Trina!" she called. But Trina was already out the door.

Probably going off for a walk alone, Erin thought. Trina was always doing that back at Sunnyside, when something was bothering her.

She started up the stairs. Sarah was on her way down. "There are cookies in the kitchen," Erin told her.

"Thanks," Sarah said, brushing past her. At the top of the stairs, Erin looked back. Sarah wasn't going toward the kitchen. She was getting her coat out of the hall closet.

Erin guessed that she was going to the library. When Sarah was feeling down, she read. Erin never could understand how reading could cheer a person up.

She was up on the second floor landing when Megan came out of her bedroom. "Erin, do you have any envelopes?" she asked.

"Look in my father's study," Erin said. "On his desk." Megan disappeared down the hall.

Erin paused before Katie's room, and looked inside. Katie was sitting on the bed. Spread out in front of her were all the gifts she had bought, neatly wrapped in colorful paper and ribbons.

"What are you doing?" Erin asked.

"Just thinking," Katie replied. "You know, not one person in my family really needs any of this stuff."

"You don't have to give practical gifts for Christmas," Erin pointed out.

Katie didn't respond. Erin withdrew and went down the hall to her own room. There, she flung herself on the bed. Going to that shelter was a big mistake, she decided. That experience had absolutely killed everyone's holiday spirit.

Including her own. Now, all she could think about was Woody, stuck in that place. At least now the mystery of him was resolved. Everything made sense. He hadn't eaten lunch or wanted to go to the movies because he had no money. The shabby clothes and the hole in his sweater—they weren't a fashion statement. Collecting the cans and bottles . . . maybe he did care about the environment, but he also needed the money he'd get for them.

She reached for the phone and dialed the shelter again. This time, she heard a series of odd clicks. And then a mechanical recorded voice announced, "The number you have dialed is temporarily out of order."

A dull realization hit her. She was going to have to go back to that awful place. She dragged herself off the bed and went out in the hall. She was about to ask Katie and Megan if they'd go with her, but she changed her mind. There was no point in making them even more depressed than they already were. If she left them alone, maybe by tonight they'd be over their gloom and they could all have some fun again.

So she slipped by their rooms, went downstairs, and got her coat. Outside, she walked slowly. Once she reached a street that had some shops, she paused before each one, examining whatever items stood in the windows. She thought that maybe buying something would cheer her up—it usually did. But nothing seemed the least bit tempting.

The ugly brick building loomed before her. Erin squared her shoulders. The sooner she went in, the sooner she could get out. She certainly didn't want to linger in front of it—she might run into Woody. Knowing what she did about him now, she wouldn't know what to say to him.

Joyce and Sandy were both behind the desk in the reception area. And they both seemed surprised to see Erin.

"I didn't expect to see *you* here again too," Joyce remarked.

Erin didn't know what Joyce meant by "too," but she didn't waste time asking. "I just have a message for a woman here." Before she got any farther, she heard the door behind her open. From Joyce's and Sandy's expressions, she could see that whoever was there wasn't expected either.

Erin turned around. Two men were coming in. One was lugging a huge fir tree. The other held boxes. "What's this?" Sandy asked.

"It's a Christmas tree, lady," one of the men said. "Where do you want it?"

The other man rested the boxes on the desk. "These are decorations."

"But who sent this?" Joyce asked in bewilderment.

The answer to that question came in the door. "Trina!" Erin exclaimed.

Trina smiled shyly. "I thought you might like this," she told the women. "I know it's not the most important thing you need, but it might make the children feel a little better."

"It's wonderful!" Joyce cried out. "Let's set it up in the main room." Sandy opened one of the boxes, and exclaimed in pleasure over the array of colorful ornaments.

Erin went over to Trina. "That must have been expensive. I thought you'd spent all your money."

"I did," Trina admitted. "I went back to the mall and returned the camera."

Erin was astonished. "But you needed that camera! You said you want to be a professional photographer."

"Yeah, I do," Trina said. "But right now I'm just an amateur. I didn't need such a fancy camera."

They could hear the cries of delight from the main room as the two women dragged the tree in. Trina and Erin followed them. The residents of the shelter were gathering around the tree. To their surprise, Sarah was with them.

"What are you doing here?" Erin asked.

"I finally thought of something worth spending my essay prize money on," Sarah told them. She pointed to a chair, on which lay a stack of thick blankets. "You want to help me put these on the beds?"

Joyce turned to Sandy. "We should go next door

and invite the men. We can have a tree-decorating party!"

Oh no, Erin thought. Woody might come. She had to get out of there. She headed toward the door, which opened before she reached it. She bumped smack into Katie.

"Hi," Katie said casually, as if she'd expected to find them all there. "Oh good, you've got a tree. Now there's something for me to put this stuff under." She was carrying a big bag.

"What's in there?" Erin asked.

"Toys, for the kids here. I returned all the stuff I bought."

"But what about the Christmas gifts for your family?"

Katie gave a nonchalant shrug. "I think the folks here need Christmas presents more than my parents and brothers do. Or me either."

Erin watched the door nervously. A couple of men were coming in. She hurried past them. In the reception area, another surprise awaited her.

Megan was at the desk, addressing envelopes. In front of her was the list of each person she had to buy a Christmas gift for and the amount of money she wanted to spend on each one.

She grinned when she saw Erin. "Now I don't have to worry about finding something for each person that costs exactly the right amount."

"What are you talking about?" Erin asked.

"See? I wanted to spend ten dollars on my aunt. So I'm giving the ten dollars in my aunt's name to the shelter and sending her one of these thank you cards. And I can do the same thing for every person on my list!" Her eyes shifted, and she looked past Erin. "Oh, hi, Woody."

Erin experienced a sickening sensation in the pit of her stomach. Slowly, she turned around.

Woody was pale. "What are you doing here?"

Behind Erin, Joyce came into the area with Sarah and Trina. "Hi, Woody," they chorused as they picked up the boxes of ornaments.

"Isn't this great?" Joyce said to Woody. "The girls have brought a tree, and blankets, and gifts. I hope your mother and Colleen come back from their walk soon. We're going to decorate the tree."

Woody was speechless. His eyes darted from one girl to the other. They rested on Erin. Then he turned around and walked outside.

Erin ran after him, pulling her coat tighter against the cold. Woody was headed toward the door to the men's side. "Woody, wait! Please!"

He stopped and faced her, but his expression was cold. "How did you find out?" he asked bluntly.

"We followed you here this morning," Erin confessed.

"Why?"

Erin was too nervous to come up with a good lie. She fumbled with her words. "Well, you were so mysterious, and—and Trina saw you take the peanut butter . . ."

He flushed. "Okay, I'm a thief, and you want

**115**

your peanut butter back. Well, don't worry, you'll get it. As soon as I collect some more bottles, I'll give you the money for it. And I wouldn't have taken it in the first place, except that peanut butter is just about the only thing my kid sister eats, and they don't have any here."

"I don't care about the peanut butter!" Erin exclaimed. "I was curious about you because . . . because . . ."

"Because why?"

"Because you didn't ask me out! And I wanted to know why, because I liked you!"

Woody gazed at her evenly. "Okay, I'll tell you why. If I asked you out, sooner or later you'd find out that I'm homeless. You wouldn't want anything more to do with me."

"How do you know I wouldn't" Erin challenged him.

"How many homeless guys do you go out with?" he shot back.

"None," she replied honestly. "I've never known anyone who was homeless before." Her voice softened. "It must be awful."

His eyes narrowed. "I don't need your pity."

"Have you been here a long time?" she asked.

"A week." He paused. "Okay, I'll satisfy your curiosity, and then maybe you'll leave. My father . . . well, never mind the reason, but he left us. My mother lost her job. Then our house caught fire, and it was totally destroyed. We found out afterwards that the insurance had run out. So that was

**116**

it. No home, no money." His voice cracked, and he turned away.

Erin was glad he turned away from her. She'd never seen such pain on a person's face before, and it was almost unbearable to witness. She was relieved to see his mother and little sister coming up the street toward them.

"Woody, hi," his mother called. "Why, hello again," she said to Erin. "Do you two know each other?"

The door to the shelter opened, and Trina put her head out. "Colleen, come help decorate the Christmas tree!"

"A Christmas tree!" Colleen yelled. "Yay!" She ran into the shelter.

Woody's mother seemed surprised. "There's a Christmas tree inside?"

"Yeah," Woody muttered. "Erin and her friends are into giving to the poor and needy. I guess it makes them feel noble or something."

"Woody, don't talk like that," his mother chided him. "People want to be kind. We'd be doing the same for others, if we could."

"Actually, I didn't bring anything," Erin said. "I came to see you."

"Me?" the woman asked.

"Yes. You said you were looking for a job and you used to be a French teacher. My father needs someone in his office who can read French and translate stuff for him. He said he could see you tomorrow morning if you're interested."

"That's wonderful!" the woman cried out.

Woody didn't seem to think so. "We don't want your charity," he barked.

"It's not charity, it's a job," his mother retorted. "And that's something I want and need very much. Once I have a job, we can get an apartment and start making a decent life for ourselves again."

Erin took a card out of her pocketbook. "Here's the address of my father's company and the phone number. If you want, you can call him now and make an appointment."

"Thank you very much, dear. I'm going to call him right this minute." She leaned over and kissed Erin's cheek. "Woody, you'd better be nice to this girl. I think she's a special person."

Erin felt oddly dizzy. She *did* feel special, more special than she felt when she wore a new dress or got lots of compliments. But did Woody think she was special too?

Woody stared at the ground. Erin shifted her weight from one leg to the other. Then she said, "Well, I guess I'll go now. It's cold out here."

Woody looked up. "Do you want to know why I carry this knapsack everywhere?"

"If you want to tell me," Erin replied.

"Because these shelters aren't exactly the safest places in the world. And everything I own in the world is in this knapsack. It's not much, just a book and some underwear. But sometimes a real pathetic character shows up here, someone who's

**118**

desperate enough to take anything that's lying around. So I can't let it out of my sight."

Erin swallowed. "I see."

"And you want to know why you saw me sleeping at the bus station? Because sometimes a couple of drunks come in here at night, and make so much noise I can't get any sleep."

Erin was suddenly aware that her eyes were wet. She thought of her own home, with all its comfort and warmth, with plenty of food and everything else anyone could desire. All those things she'd taken for granted. And she compared her life with Woody's life.

She fought back the tears. They would only make Woody realize how sorry she felt for him, and his pride would suffer. He'd be furious with her. But despite her efforts, a tear trickled down her face.

Woody couldn't miss it. But he didn't get angry. He spoke in a low voice. "I know I should apologize," he said. "It's not your fault that I'm here. And it's nice, what you and your friends are doing. I guess I was just taking my frustration out on you."

"That's okay," Erin said. "I know it wasn't personal. You could have been angry at Trina or Katie or—"

"No," Woody interrupted. "You're the one that makes me feel the worst."

"Why?"

"Because I did want to ask you out. And I couldn't. I had no money to take you out with.

Besides, I didn't want you to get to know me too well. Because you'd find out the truth about me."

Erin nodded. It all made sense to her now. She tried a small smile. "Maybe your mother will get that job tomorrow. And then, like she said, you'll be able to get a home."

"And then I could ask you out?"

Erin let the smile widen. "You could ask me out right now. This is the 1990s, Woody. Boys don't have to pay for dates all the time."

She thought she had stopped crying, but there was still something wet on her cheeks. She looked up. "Hey, it's started snowing."

"Yeah," he said. "Let's go check out that tree."

Inside the shelter, the tree was all decorated. Trina, Katie, Megan and Sarah were entertaining the residents with Christmas carols. Erin and Woody joined them.

His mother came over to them. "I just spoke with your father," she said to Erin. Her face was glowing. "The job in his office sounds absolutely perfect for me. And he's going to see me first thing in the morning." She put an arm around her son. "Oh, Woody, just think. We might be spending Christmas day in our own home!"

"Yeah," Woody said. "That would be great." He spoke quietly, but Erin didn't miss the light that came into his eyes. Nor did she fail to notice that his hand was now covering hers.

A man appeared at the door. "Did someone here order ten pizzas?"

Joyce and Sandy stared at him in consternation. "Ten pizzas!" they said in unison.

"I ordered them," Megan piped up. She ran to the man and pulled money from her pocket. "They're my parents' Christmas gift."

She got puzzled looks from everyone except the cabin six girls. They spread the pizzas out on a table, everyone dug in, and soon the atmosphere was positively festive.

"I guess pizza isn't exactly Christmas food," Megan said. "But it was the only place that would deliver."

"It tastes Christmassy to me," Katie declared.

Sandy came up to them. "I want to thank all you girls. This is a very fine thing you've done."

Trina gazed around the room sadly. "It's just pizza and a Christmas tree, and some blankets and gifts. It's not going to solve their problems."

"No, you're right," Sandy said. "But you've helped make their day a little brighter."

"And that's what Sunnyside girls are supposed to do," Sarah noted.

Erin's forehead puckered. "Huh?"

"You remember," Sarah said. "Every summer, Ms. Winkle makes that tired old speech about how a Sunnyside girl is supposed to bring a little sunshine wherever she goes."

"Oh yeah, I remember," Erin said. "And I remember how we used to make those faces every time she said that."

"And laugh," Katie added. Her expression became thoughtful. "But you know what? I'm feeling like maybe this is what she meant, like we've just discovered what she was talking about. I know that sounds corny," she added hastily.

"It's not corny," Trina said. "And I think we've discovered something else too."

"What's that?" Megan asked.

"What Christmas is all about."

Erin looked around. The people she saw looked a little less sad, a little more optimistic. After Christmas would come a new year, and maybe the new year would find all these people in happier circumstances.

She looked at Woody. The despair she'd seen in his eyes was gone. It had been replaced with hope. And when he squeezed her hand, she felt a rush of happiness. Now she had her own personal hope for the new year!

Everyone was singing now, a rousing chorus of "Joy to the World." Katie edged closer to Erin.

"You know what this reminds me of? A Sunnyside camp fire."

Erin rolled her eyes. "Katie, we don't sing 'Joy to the World' at Sunnyside camp fires."

"I know that," Katie replied indignantly. "But it's the same feeling. You know what I mean?"

Erin looked around at her cabin mates and at all the others in the room. She saw their eyes shining with wishes and dreams and hope for the future.

And she knew what Katie meant.